THE HOSPITAL
STEWARD

THE HOSPITAL STEWARD

A Western Medical Fiction circa 1930-1950 Romance and Entrepreneur

A SEQUEL—BOOK 2

Richard M Beloin MD

Rev. date: 08/14/2024

To order additional copies of this book, contact:
Xlibris
844-714-8691
www.Xlibris.com
Orders@Xlibris.com
861892

CONTENTS

CONTENTS

AUTHOR'S DISCLAIMER

A Disclaimer

This is a work of fiction. Names, characters, business events, and products are all the result of the writer's imagination. Any resemblance to actual events, people, and locations are purely coincidental.

Some of my stories occur during well documented historical events such as the 1918 Influenza, WW1, the Roaring 20's, and so on. It is again coincidental that this story occurs during these times, but the story itself does not alter the historical facts.

DEDICATION

This sequel is dedicated to my old patients who did not have to deal with developing medicine and surgery some100 years ago. They had the luxury of modern medicine of the mid-70s to the mid-90s.

PREFACE

It is no surprise to our readers that a sequel would follow to the original 'The New Western Doctor.' It is now 1930 and the next generation of Kelly doctors and their doctor wives are returning to their hometown to continue delivering medical care. Along with their parents the teams will go thru the Great Depression, the New Deal, the oppressive polio epidemic, and the offensive Germans in WWII. The facts revealed about those times, especially the treatment for paralyzed patients, can become a permanent implant into your memory.

Before the story starts, I will review the original story in a prologue. That way, the current story of 'The Hospital Steward' will become a standalone publication.

Author, Richard M Beloin MD

PROLOGUE

Doctor Brad Kelly was wool gathering while riding along the river. He had to make an existential decision as he saw a nude woman frantically trying to stay afloat as a wall of mud was on her tail. He presumed that the gal got caught in a blown-out dam upriver. Reacting quickly he was able to pull the drowning gal to shore.

After spending a few days getting acquainted, he told the gal he was a physician and had come to town to open a hospital. After a week of an accelerated romance, the two got married. After a honeymoon, the Duo made arrangements to start building their memorial hospital and then headed to Dallas for training—Brad in surgery, and Addie in nursing.

The Duo then went thru some grueling loops of study, work, and lack of sleep. Addie was a charismatic, polite, and volunteering student who worked hard studying and never shrugged any assignment as difficult or as less appealing as it could be. After excelling prematurely in general nursing, she was promoted to OR nurse assigned to controlling surgical instruments during surgery. In time she was promoted to a surgeon's assistant—reaching her goal of assisting her surgical husband a distinct likelihood.

Brad was a natural talent in surgery. His skills were quickly recognized as he sailed thru the surgical training. After performing the required dozen major procedures as the surgeon in charge, he quickly became a surgical attending and was able to schedule his own cases and have his wife as the assistant surgeon.

All thru their training they periodically went back to their hometown of Amarillo to check on the hospital's progress. At the same time they became friends with other students in the surgical and nursing programs. At the end of training the Duo made their way back to Texas along with three other doctors and their nursing wives—another general surgeon Tom

Hall MD, an obstetrician Stanley Norwood MD, and a pathologist Daniel Greene MD. It was 1905 and it was time to establish their practice.

With some expected growing pains, the group of medical providers walked right into the golden years as their practice flourished. Things took a abrupt change when the US entered WWI. First they lost Doctor Hall to the medical corps—a volunteer general surgeon who requested an assignment as a receiving field hospital surgeon. Doctor Hall was fortunate to learn military techniques for saving soldiers' lives. As the war ended, he returned to the Kelly Hospital with new methods in handling trauma victims.

During the war the need for medical services slowed down. When it became clear that an influenza pandemic would follow the war, the Duo acted and built a new wing to the hospital for the specific purpose of treating the most ill of influenza patients. After a year of using the new wing, it was closed as the pandemic resolved. The treatments they provided saved all but 4% of the sickest patients to include dehydrated and or pneumonia patients.

When the Roaring 20s arrived, the hospital practice again flourished as Addie had pushed the doctors to get more specialized training. Doctor Hall added Urology as Doctor Scanlon added Orthopedics, and Doctor Kelly added vascular surgery. These specialties brought patients from New Mexico to the west, Oklahoma to the east, and Colorado to the north.

In 1924 the two Kelly kids and their high school sweethearts elected to go to medical school to become medical doctors. The two men also added two years for surgical training. It was another time when the hospital flourished until that infamous day in October 1929 when the stock market crashed and plunged the country in the Great Depression of the 30s.

As the story came to an end, it was clear that the next generation of Kelly doctors would be the ones to carry the Kelly Memorial Hospital thru the next decade and into the future.

THE STORY NOW CONTINUES!

CHAPTER 1

The Early 30s

It had been two weeks since the October stock market crash when Brad and Addie had an old appointment with Mike Walters, the local carpenter. "Well, since you scheduled this meeting, I suspect you want renovations, more hospital storage, or new houses for the incoming doctors—so which one is it?" Addie said, "we wanted two more doctor houses on Doctor's Row and two more car garages." Brad added, "but seeing the country in a depression, maybe we should cancel our plans and try to fine some apartments for our two kids and their spouses."

Mike was surprised and said, "you may not believe this but it is the best time to build. The stock market crash caught all our merchants by surprise with an overstocked inventory. Since the banks are not giving out building loans, cash is king. If you have the cash, you will likely end up with a 10% discount for two houses and two garages. Plus the stores are full to include the hardware stores, the lumber yards, the furniture stores, the plumbing/electrical and heating stores. As long as you take the items in their stores. If you want something else that requires an order, then you will not get it, since nationwide manufacturing is nonexistent."

"Really, well in that case, how much will it cost us to build both houses and garages?" "I anticipated your request, so I checked the last Doctor's Row house we built for you, added current prices for materials, and it looks like we can build all four buildings for a flat rate of $4,000 as long as we do not finish the second floor except for the second water closet upstairs." The Duo both said, "then go ahead and start." "Great, we have six weeks to be enclosed before the winter, and all winter to do the interior finish work." "Our kids will arrive by mid-April, can you be done by then?" "Absolutely, we'll even have the lawns seeded by then." "When can you start?" "Tomorrow morning we'll be laying down concrete!"

*

The month to Xmas was a subdued time. For some strange reason, no one was sick, doctor's offices were quiet, and hospital patients were rare except for heart attacks, attempted suicide, car accidents, farm injuries, or emergency surgery. The hospital's yearly party was cancelled and only skeletal crews of nurses and ancillary staff were kept on as the others were on standby. It was Xmas night when the Duo was having an emergency private meeting in their extra-large bathtub.

It was Brad who started the discussion. "Tell me dear, how much do we have in the hospital fund to continue covering expenses, and what administrative miracle are you planning to save our hospital in the coming months?" "Well first of all let's start with the emergency fund. We have $40,000 in cash in our walk-in-vault for this purpose. Now predicting how long that will last is a real crapshoot since there will always be some income from our hospitalized patients. Office income and surgical fees belong to the doctors and are not used to cover hospital expenses. Now I have worked the figures every which way and used my crystal ball to predict that we can maintain the status quo till the next election of 1932."

"Now pray tell dear, why does the election have anything to do with our hospital's survival?" "Well dear, our current Republican President Herbert Hoover believes that the depression will run its course in due time. Whereas the democratic candidate, by the name of Franklin Delano Roosevelt believes that major social changes will be needed to get the country out of the depression. He is talking about employing men to build the country's infrastructure, federally insuring bank deposits, adding controls on the stock market, controlling farm prices, cancelling prohibition while adding liquor taxes for federal income, and adding social security employment taxes for guaranteeing individual retirement income."

"But how is all this going to help hospitals?" "Economy is a trickle- down effect. If the country and people are doing well, the use of hospitals for elective and referral surgery will resume to pre stock market crash levels." "Ok, but what can be done to increase hospital income before the next national election?" "I have been working on this and come up with two things: local town council subsidies and prepaid hospital insurance!" "My dear wife, we all know how council subsidies are like pulling teeth from a mad dog and with no money or major manufacturing jobs; who can afford prepaid insurance?"

"Hear me out, dear. Let's start with prepaid hospital insurance. We have documented evidence that it can work. Right here in Dallas, the Baylor Plan was put into practice. Using the working class, 1500 public school teachers were given 21 days of prepaid hospital days at a cost to the employer of $6 per year per teacher: or at a cost of $9,000 (1500 X 6) per employer. With divided monthly payments, the employer was able to meet his financial responsibilities. This system of pre-payment for individual workers is called capitation."

"The only problem was it did not cover for children, spouses, elderly, or minority groups especially the Negroes. Now today we can offer a local employer the same deal as the Baylor Plan offered." "But dear, no one is working and so who can pay a capitation fee?" "We have one employer who can—the railroad and we can make it more appealing by including spouses and dependent children." "Well I agree and I want to be on that meeting when you make an offer to the railroad manager."

"Now as far as subsidies go from the town council, what can you use as unusual times as we had during the 1918 pandemic?" "But dear, we are just beginning our current epidemic, the polio epidemic, heh? When you hear what it will cost us to treat these patients, you will not hesitate to ask for public subsidies!"

"So we have town subsidies, prepaid hospital insurance, and last year's profit in our vault as the current stabilization factors, any other?" "Yes, I have filed our federal tax status from private to non-profit. That will save us 15% in taxes or +-$6,000. That means that we have to spend last year's $40,000 profit during the current year, and probably extend it over the next two years as we use it to keep our hospital open. That is a start and I am working on other solutions. Those are still in the embryonic stages and we'll discuss them at a later date. Now my hormones are working overtime and I am not in a sexual embryonic stage. So lend me your accessory before I scream!"

*

The next month saw no changes. Emergency medical surgeries, accident treatment, and heart attacks maintained minimal hospital activities with the use of nurses and ancillary services kept at a minimum. Outlying referrals for specific surgery were still nonexistent. Feeling the pressure to guarantee a minimal hospital income, the Duo arranged for a meeting with the new Amarillo railroad station manager: Benjamin True.

After introductions, it was clear to the Duo that they were dealing with a domineering manager who practiced arrogant control to its maximum. "So what can I do for you as the local hospital managers?" Addie quickly added, "we are not managers, we own this hospital—your only local medical care for this small city, this double county of Randall and Potter, and this actual 26 counties in the Texas Panhandle. To be even more specific, we draw from the entire 25,000 square miles that make up the panhandle and its estimated 95,000 people." Brad added, "and the railroad has thousands of track miles in the panhandle with an estimated 500 employees. Consequently we are here to discuss prepaid hospital insurance, prepaid doctor's office visits, and prepaid surgical fees."

Manager True lost it and started laughing. "Ha-ha-ha-haah. Since you are the only medical care in the panhandle, all our employees need to do is show up and you cannot refuse us. Ha-ha-ha-haah! So why on earth should the railroad give you a penny ahead of provided services?. What is wrong with the old standard of fee for service?"

Addie took over and said, "because in the long run it will cost you two to three times more than prepaid care based on capitation. Are you aware of the Baylor Plan?" "Yes, of course!" "Well we are offering you a similar plan but in three phases. For your 500 employees, we are offering each worker a total of 24 days of prepaid hospital days for $8 a year per worker, or $4,000 plus a once in a lifetime maximum of two months of prepaid care for life threatening illnesses. For office visits, we are offering five doctor visits per year per worker for another $8 per year per worker or a yearly fee of $4,000. And last, if you want surgeon's fee coverage, each worker can have two surgical procedures, one minor and one major, per year for another $8 per year per worker or another $4,000."

Manager True was doing mental computations as he said, "so for $12,000 of prepaid insurance, my 500 railroad employees in the Texas Panhandle can each have 24 paid hospital days, five office doctor visits, and two surgical procedure, one minor and one major, per year?" "Correct!" "Seems rather high for a crap-shoot chance that each worker can use all the services." "Yes it is a gamble for you and us, that is what is called capitation and not a crap-shoot."

The manager thought he had the advantage when he asked, "give me examples of events that would affect my entire workforce." Brad took over and said, "a polio epidemic has started in the larger Texas cities and the nearest is Dallas only 350 miles away. An adult who is paralyzed from the polio virus could spend months in the hospital and could use up their once in a lifetime maximum of two month's stay without any costs."

"Well, I'll believe we'll get a polio epidemic when it happens." Addie was not going to be outdone as she adds, "what will happen if your train has a derailment and 150 passengers/workers appear in our emergency room. Where else can any system handle such a medical catastrophe. It sounds to me that free medical care is a mitigation against hundreds of lawsuits, heh" The manager was pensive and sat back in his chair. That is when Addie gave the 'coup-de-grâce,' "today only, as a bonus for you signing up on all three prepaid plans, we will include all victims of a train derailment for the next year and will accept your monthly payment of $1,000 starting today; if we sign the contract before we leave your office."

Manager True kept looking at both Addie and Brad. It was clear that he had been outmaneuvered by two experts. To save face, he pulled out a bank draft book and made a $1,000 draft payable to the Kelly Hospital. The only words the manager said were, "I am certain that you have a premade contract, please hand it over so we can cut off the diseased limb, and bring this pain to an end, heh?"

As they were leaving the manager asked, "would you have refused to treat railroad workers without that contract in your hands?" "There is an element of hospital ownership that must be respected. That is why I am the functioning administrator and Doctor Kelly is the Chief of Medical Staff—as it is my duty to be firm to guarantee the hospital's survival as Doctor Kelly guarantees quality medical care. With that in mind, I guess it is theoretical and we may never know the true answer to your question, heh?"

*

Addie was proud as a peacock as they walked back to the hospital. It was Brad who asked, "are we really expecting another epidemic with this polio virus?" "From my reading it is a matter of time before Amarillo is hit and it is expected to last a decade or more unless a vaccine is made to provide immunity against this virus." Walking in front of the telegraph office, Addie said, "let's stop and check for telegrams." Brad sat outside on the bench as Addie went inside. Addie was slow to come out and when she did, she handed Brad a telegram letter. "Speaking of the polio epidemic, you'd better read this letter from Dottie." Brad read the letter and when finished said, "it is now clear to me that the writing is on the wall. An epidemic is on its way and we need the tools to fight it. So place a $10,000 order thru the distribution center in Houston and pray God that we can wait the six weeks to get our order."

Ironically, it was also six weeks away when the Quad of new doctors were expected. The Duo was making preparations to include finishing the two houses with garages, rearranging the old medical ward for the new polio center, and writing continuing education programs to prepare the entire hospital and medical staff to deal with what was coming—polio.

It was now days before the Quad arrived and the Duo was having their monthly private hot tub meeting. Brad started, "well dear your prepaid medical plan has been active for over a month. Do you have any statistics as to whether the railroad used up their $1,000 monthly capitation fee?" "Why of course, I would not dare come to this meeting without the facts. So I excluded the first two weeks as startup time. In the last month I have tabulated the number of office visits, the number of used hospital days, and the number of minor and major surgeries. Had these services been paid 100% in cash, the bill would have come to $650."

"So we are ahead this month with the railroad using up 65% of benefits!" "Yes but I am expecting that the usage will plateau at 75% unless we have a dreaded railroad catastrophe and need to pull a Code D." "Well, until that happens, if it does, we will deal with it, heh?" "All in all, I firmly believe that it is best for everyone to be working even if it is out of our capitation fees—especially with the four kids about to get on board,"

Addie then added, "speaking of money, what are we planning on paying the four doctors when they go to work?" Brad thought a bit and finally said, "had you asked me that question before the October crash I would have said $5,500 per year for surgeons and $4,500 for medical doctors. Now in the middle of this depression I am not sure. What do you think?" "Looking back, years ago, when the kids entered medical school, they made it clear that they would come back to us and join us in our practice. Money was never discussed. Today I agree that income has crashed during this depression. That should not alter our commitment to them. We built them new houses as we should give them a salary consistent with the times—before the crash. Plus we will fill their larder with food and add the new cars in the garages—one a Ford Fordor Series and the other a Chevrolet Master Series and both as a two-door coupe. Now was that a sublimal suggestion regards birth control?" "Hey, if they decide to start a family they will need to trade vehicles for a four-door sedan and pay for it themselves."

"Well getting back to the kids' income, their biweekly pay will be: for the surgeons $212 and for the medical doctors $173. Unless you want to give them equal pay?" "No, I am certain that the standard has already been established and we should continue it as a matter of reality—surgeons do generate a higher income." Brad asked, "should we give them a sign-on bonus?" "No, the 2-door coupe is their $750 bonus, heh?"

"The only other issue is where we take the money to pay their salaries. Do we take it out of the hospital fund or our personal stash of cash?" "When it comes to money, I defer to you." Addie thought about it and finally said, "for nearly twenty-five years we have been saving for our retirement. We have more money than we will ever be able to spend. Once we are gone, they will all inherit the left-over money. So why tax the hospital fund, let's take their salary out of our personal vault." "Sounds good to me!"

*

It was two days before the Quad arrived that JD came rushing into Addie's office. "Hey boss, the railroad just delivered six huge wooden crates each weighing over 400 pounds, three smaller crates weighing 50 pounds, and several boxes labeled parts to assemble. The problem is that I did not order them, did you?" "Do the crates say, 'made by Emerson Co. of Cambridge, Mass?'" "Yes!" "Then break the boxes open and start assembling each unit. Once operational, wheel each unit to the polio center which was the original six bed unit in the medical ward."

The day finally arrived as six nervous parents were waiting at the railroad platform. With the train coming to a stop, it seemed forever for passengers to start stepping out. It was Addie who saw Dottie first appear. The two ran to each other and the tears started flowing. One by one, the other three appeared and the greetings were filled with smiles and tears. At one point Dottie asked her mom, "have the units arrived yet?" "Yes, two days ago. JD, our purchasing agent has five assembled and is working on the sixth today. Tomorrow, he assembles the three rocking beds." "Good then in two days, let's plan on having a day of continuing education. We'll do the evening and night shift in the morning, and the day shift in the afternoon. Doctors and ancillary staff can choose their time to attend. Susie will give the lecture on polio and I will start the demonstration of the 'iron lung.' We will then share the discussion of how to operate the 'iron lung' till everyone knows how these units work."

Addie was surprised and asked, "are we close to getting our first cases of polio?" Dottie answered, "since Xmas, the medical clinic where we worked all year was closed because of the depression. So Susie and I volunteered in the polio breathing center. For three months we cared for paralyzed patients as we worked rotating between day, evening, and night shifts. I can attest to the fact that when we left Dallas, they had six long term cases in the iron lung and were getting new cases each day. Dallas, Oklahoma City, Alburquerque, and Pueblo are only +- 300 miles from here so we better plan on being ready as soon as possible."

**

CHAPTER 2

Another Epidemic

That evening was spent in the Duo's parlor. It was mostly a nostalgic review of past years from the high school years to 4-6 years of medical/surgical training. Fortunately, medicine was not the subject at hand. Instead it was the personal living situation that they had endured during those training years. Early in the evening, the Quad was introduced to their new home and their first car.

Morning found everyone at church services followed by a full dinner in the hospital cafeteria. After their meal, the Quad started talking about the new things in surgery. Jimmy started, "there are many new synthetic sutures, absorbable and nonabsorbable, coming out soon that we will need to get used to. But the big thing is a dye that is used in common duct exploration beyond the old-style probing. With a portable X Ray machine we can fill the common duct with the dye and see any residual stones."

Eric jumped in and said, "the nicest invention is electrocautery to buzz bleeders without tying them off. The problem is that it cannot be used with the new flammable anesthesia gases of ethylene, cyclopropane, and divinyl ether. It can only be used with chloroform, nitrous oxide, or the new trichlorethylene. You'll love to use it as it is much faster and leaves less sutures in the surgical wounds as a nidus for infections."

Jimmy resumed and said, "we are now trained in trepanation. For gunshots to the head, we can remove a part of the skull to tie off bleeders and debride dead brain tissues. After doing the work, the skull plate is replaced and covered with scalp. If there is brain edema, the skull flap can lift up and we now use diuretic injections to control edema. Post op seizures are common and we treat them with barbiturates and supplemental oxygen. For closed head trauma with brain swelling we can do a craniectomy to reduce high pressure brain damage."

Brad and Tom were very attentive as Brad asked, "what is new in vascular surgery?" Jimmy jumped on that one, "coming soon is an anticoagulant called heparin which will keep your temporary carotid bypass open. It will allow the new fem-fem and fem-pop bypasses once they manufacture some synthetic tubing for permanent use."

Eric then added, "of course we now have penicillin and sulfa antibiotics to fight infection. Sulfa is cheap but penicillin G is rather expensive at $100 for 100,000 units which is a very small dose. Of course the sulfa drugs are popular in urological instrumentation to prevent post-op urosepsis. The newest finding is to extensively debride wounds and remove all borderline tissues that are the main nidus for infections."

Addie had been listening but needed to know something, "which specialty will you and Eric be more interested in?" Jimmy answered, "I want to be involved in vascular surgery and trepanation (neurosurgery)." Eric quickly added, "I am like Dad,

I like minimally invasive surgery with the cystoscope, the prostate resectoscope, and the ureter catheters to pull out stones. I have been working with the Dallas urologists and have a few new techniques to share with dad."

There was a long pause as Brad said, "well what is new with you ladies and what departments will you specialize in?" Dottie started, "we have discussed this and we will be specializing in the following:

GENERAL MEDICINE. "We will be introducing new drugs.

Aspirin has been proven to decrease platelet adhesiveness and decrease the chance of angina progressing to a heart attack.

Insulin or Metrazol shock for schizophrenia treatment.

Amphetamines for fatigue, low blood pressure, or depression.

Quinine for malaria.

Colchicine for arthritis."

VACCINATION CLINICS. "Susie has been in contact with Doctor Hallet who is the panhandle health commissioner. With 26 counties and a total population in 1930 of +-95,000 people, there is a need for establishing vaccination clinics. We have agreed on a fee for either Susie or me of $40 a day for six-hour clinics held in the town hall. We would vaccinate against smallpox, diphtheria, pertussis, tetanus, and yellow fever."

CCU/ICU. "We both spent a lot of time in the CCU and the very ill in the ICU. Although we still do not have a reliable defibrillator or heart monitor, we do have alarms that pick up extremely slow or fast heartbeats that usually warn of complications. As of now, all heart attacks or intractable angina are placed on aspirin, procain, sublingual nitroglycerin and oxygen. We have several drugs to treat complications of heart attacks:

Bradycardia—epinephrine injections.

Atrial Fibrillation--digitalis.

Congestive heart failure—mercurial diuretic injections.

Tachycardia—barbiturates.

Ventricular ectopy—higher doses of procain.

Cardiac arrest—epinephrine and CPR.

Ventricular tachycardia or fibrillation—precordial thump and CPR."

POLIO. "We both plan to be heavily involved in treating the paralyzed patients in the acute phase while in the 'iron lung' and afterwards in the rocking beds, and post discharge outpatient physical therapy visits. Just so you know, we have applied for funds from federal agencies to include UNICEF, the March of Dimes, and the Federal Health Agency that covers the 26 counties in the Texas Panhandle. Whether or not if these agencies pan out, only time will tell."

Before the meeting broke up, Addie gave each new doctor their assignments in case of a Code D with the special notation that "a call of a Code D is not a practice—it is a real catastrophe."

*

Two days later, arrangements were made for outside invitees and the hospital's evening and night shift nurses and ancillary staff to attend a lecture on polio and the treatment of the severely affected.

Outside invitees included: Mayor Monroe, the four-member city council with Murdock Hatfield as the president, Judge Gagnon as the Potter County representative, Sheriff Butler, city philanthropist Mister Gregory, the well-known panhandle health commissioner, Doctor Hallet, the school principal Winston MacBride, Mike Walters the contractor, and the local methodist minister Pastor Tillotson. As a professional courtesy for 500 prepaid health customers, Benjamin True was present as the local railroad manager. The remainder of the class in attendance was the evening and night shift of hospital workers, and all the doctors on medical staff.

The meeting was held in the cafeteria and Dottie started the process.

"Welcome doctors, invitees, and hospital staff. Doctor Kelly and I will do a presentation and will then have a Q&A session to answer all your question—so hold off till our presentation is done. We are here to learn about another epidemic that will soon appear in our community. Unlike the Influenza of 1918 which hit hard, caused towns to shut down, and this hospital treated hundreds over two months; the epidemic was over in one year. The polio epidemic will hit in small local attacks all over the country and will be recurrent many times a year over predicted decades. Yes, that is correct when I say 'on and off' over the next decades."

Susie took over. "Polio is caused by a virus like the Influenza virus. Despite having two antibiotics, it is not affected by penicillin or sulfa antibiotics. An antiviral drug is probably 50 years away. There are four degrees of involvement.

"1st degree is a flu like illness to include fever, fatigue, vomiting, headaches, muscle aches, and neck stiffness. There is no specific treatment except supportive care. Fortunately most cases will be in this category."

"2nd degree is more serious and involves infiltration of the spinal cord with the virus. This causes varying degrees of paralysis of arms, legs, and intercostal muscles of breathing."

"3rd degree is very serious and involves the infiltration of the brainstem with the virus. This is called bulbar polio and causes paralysis of vocal cords, muscle of swallowing, eye muscle movement, drooping eyelids, the muscles of the diaphragm that controls spontaneous breathing when asleep, and the heart to maintain a heartbeat."

"4th degree is extremely rare, serious, and involves the brain to cause encephalitis, meningitis, delirium, coma, and death."

"Fortunately the hospital will be dealing with the second and third degrees. The expected incidence of both paralyzing categories is predicted as a minimum of 32 per 100,000 population up to as many as unknown of hundreds per 100,000 for maximum. I remind you that the panhandle has +- 95,000 people in 26 counties as Amarillo has 40,000 and the combined total of Potter and Randall counties, which encompasses Amarillo, is +- 54,000 of the panhandle's 95,000. With these statistics, the death rate for children is 2-5% whereas in adults it is 5-30%."

"The polio virus is transmitted by human-to-human transfer via the hand to mouth route. Yes the oral route is how you transmit this virus. So a person with the 1st degree flu like illness can transmit the virus in his saliva, his mouth, respiratory droplets while coughing and sneezing, and thru his feces. It is now easy to see how it can be transmitted by dirty eating utensils, lack of hand washing, drinking or bathing water laced with raw sewage, and so on. This transmission is also facilitated by gatherings of people as is seen in churches, schools, dances, other social events, meetings, playgrounds, diners and even in high-end restaurants."

Doctor Hall took the discussion further. "Let me now explain how this virus can cause paralysis. Once the virus is in your blood, it tends to infiltrate the spinal cord. There it infiltrates the motor neurons of the spinal cord. That interferes with the electrical transmission in the nerves that activate the muscles causing varying degrees of malfunctioning muscles or paralysis as we know it. How it does this is under current research but it looks like the nerve's insulating sheath is damaged. But this damaged insulation sheath can regenerate or repair itself with time but again with varying degrees of repair."

"That ends our preliminary discussion on polio and we will now take your questions. Doctor Kelly and I will alternate the answers."

Council lady—"you said we will have this affliction for likely decades to come. Well we cannot keep our kids out of school for a decade. So what are we to do?"

Doctor Susan Norwood Kelly. "As was mentioned, unlike the 1918 Influenza, this virus will hit a community in pulses instead of continuous months to a year like the 1918 epidemic. Let me give you an example.

Let's take an example of five boys presenting with paralysis. After questions revealed that all five boys, on a Saturday morning, went swimming in a popular swimming hole. Late Monday all five kids were sick and by Tuesday were developing different degrees of paralysis. Now if the council acts and closes the swimming hole down, no new cases will appear. If they don't do the deed, then the next batch of cases is on the council's shoulders. Assuming they did close it down, then the next thing to do is for the council to place the city sewage pipe downstream of the swimming hole instead of upstream as it presently is. Consequently the five-case pulse of paralytic polio is now resolved except for the weeks or months of care these five boys will need."

"Now let's take another example of six kids from the fifth grade who come down with paralytic polio. It is hoped that the school principal would close down the fifth-grade class for two to four weeks. If that does not happen, then as a parent, you need to protect your kids in that class by taking your kids out of school and 'sheltering in place' till the risk passes. During the closed time, the classroom has to be cleaned and sterilized as most of the students in the class should be checked as a possible index case—meaning the first kid who had a mild flu syndrome but infected his or her classmates. In summary, pulses of new cases can be aborted till the next pulse appears—hopefully months away!"

Mayor Monroe—what happens if there are many cases in town and you suspect the water reservoir to be the contaminated source?"

Doctor Dorothy Kelly Hall—"that is a serious matter and would be placed in the hands of the 26-county health commissioner, Doctor Hallet. The solutions range from closing down the reservoir to adding bleach to the drinking/bathing water." "Whoa, what is this about adding bleach to our city water?" Doctor Hallet answered, "municipalities all over the country are adding bleach to sterilize the water. It is the chlorine in the bleach that kills bacteria and attenuates viruses—especially the polio virus. It is added in miniscule amounts that is barely noticeable by the human palate. That is the solution for infected water reservoirs because of the raw sewage dumping in the water."

Judge Gagnon—"sounds like someone will need to do a lot of public health inquiries to find index cases or the source of contamination. Who will be assigned that thankless duty?"

Addie—"we have discussed this and if Doctors Hall and Kelly cannot be spared from the care of these victims, I will take on the responsibility."

Nurse—"can we predict how many attacks we expect for each month and how severe will the attacks be?"

Doctor Kelly—"no one knows on both count. We will be able to answer that question after a years' time. For what we experience in the total number of attacks and their severity will likely be reproduced from year to year until we get a vaccine to end this scourge." "And any idea when this vaccine might come out?" "None whatsoever."

Minister Tillotson—"this word paralysis is so frightening. Any idea of the duration of this illness and the number of patients that go home cured or have residual paralysis.

Doctor Hall—"Doctor Kelly and I have worked in the Dallas Hospital Polio Center for three + months. Holding the discussion on the treatment till the end of the Q&A session, this is what we observed:

Mild to moderate leg, arm, and chest breathing muscle paralysis—two weeks of acute treatment, 2 weeks of weaning, 2 weeks of inpatient physical therapy, and months of outpatient therapy. Of note, 1/3 of patients in this class will go home with long term residual symptoms that range in severity and require some assistive braces.

For severe 2nd degree paralysis—months of acute treatment and months of weaning with months of inpatient and outpatient therapy. Each case is different depending on the affected muscles.

For 3rd degree or bulbar polio, we have treated several in Dallas but not a one ever came off the acute treatment phase. We have no idea how long such an affliction will ravage the human body or if there is an end?

For 4th degree, no one survived."

Council President Hatfield—"going back to the water reservoir being the source of a polio outbreak, instead of spending thousands of dollars to find another water source, why couldn't we fix the problem temporarily by issuing a 'boil order' for consumption?" Doctor

Hall paused as she looked at Doctor Hallet for an answer.

Doctor Hallet—"this is what we are telling everyone in the 26 counties around Amarillo. As long as other cases do not appear, then that is Ok. If cases continue to occur, then more drastic measures may be needed."

Nurse Louisa—"Will nurses need to wear a mask and gloves to care for these patients?"

Doctor Hall—"this week we will have a training program for nurses and orderlies. All the safety instructions will be included."

Sheriff Butler—"you mentioned that a third of patients with paralysis will go home with residual symptoms. Can you be more specific?"

Doctor Kelly—"yes, first look on the bright side, 2/3 will go home without residual disease. For those affected, the residual varies from using a cane, to a leg or arm brace, to a wheelchair and so on. Some of these will eventually clear their residual symptoms with physical therapy whereas some will show the effect of old polio for life."

Nurse—"I have read that scoliosis is the frequent result of polio. Is that true?"

Doctor Hall—"yes, if the paraspinal muscles on either side of the spine are paralyzed, it is hard to do rehabilitative therapy on patients who are on their backs receiving acute treatments. More on this later under acute treatment. I may add that polio affects proximal muscles such as the upper thighs, the upper arms, the intercostal chest muscles, and the paraspinal muscles just mentioned. It does not affect the lower arms, lower legs, hands, or feet."

Mister Gregrory—"you said that a minimum of 32 patients out of the panhandle's 95,000 population will appear with significant paralysis needing acute treatment. Is this the figure you are planning on?"

Doctor Hall. "Historically, it can be up to five times as high, or up to +- 160 cases. It all depends on how strong the public health system is in our area. On that note, I assure you that we will be aggressive in identifying an index case or a new source of the virus, or getting things corrected by the powers to be, heh?"

Principal MacBride—"why is it that when five kids come down with the disease, all out of the same class, that none have the same degree of paralysis?"

Doctor Kelly—"everyone has a unique immune system that can respond to a viral infection. That in turn leads to a mild or severe affliction."

Mayor Monroe—"when we had the 1918 Influenza, this hospital treated hundreds of very sick patients and rarely did one of the care providers ever get the influenza. Could this be the same with polio?"

Doctor Hall—"yes and we hope so. Let me explain. Healthcare workers are always exposed to viruses and often get a subclinical infection that provides natural immunity. Doctor Kelly and I worked with the sickest of polio victims while in Dallas and we never experienced any symptoms, even the 1st degree flu syndrome. So we can assume that we have natural immunity as it might include this hospital's staff."

Principal MacBride—"not to beleaguer the point, but I want a clearer protocol for closing the school. Closing down a classroom was easy, but a school has many ramifications!"

Doctor Kelly—"if, as the local public health directors, we make the recommendation, you will not get any backlash. If you react by closing the school because of one classroom, then it is your prerogative to act on the side of safety. If you get backlash, bring those objecting individuals to see the patients receiving acute treatment in the polio ward. That, I assure you will shut them up!"

Nurse Louisa—"I am not clear about transmission. You claim it is a hand to mouth transmission of human to human. Yet you claim that coughing or sneezing droplets can be infectious. Can you clarify?"

Doctor Hall—"that is a tricky one. Let me say that you will not catch polio by breathing air, even if the air is packed with respiratory or nasal droplets of active cases—even the early infectious 1st degree flu syndrome. BUT, air droplets that fall on your hand and if you touch your food or mouth, you can come down with polio because you turned the air droplets in a hand to mouth transfer. Clear as mud, heh?" "No, it is finally clear and why nurses will need to wear gloves. However, if a polio victim has an apparent 'cold' you will never convince a caregiver to not wear a mask, heh?" "Probably not!"

Doctor Kelly. "We have avoided the subject of death from polio so we will now attempt to clarify the fatal mechanism."

Doctor Hall. 95% polio mortality occurs in the 3rd and 4th degree of cases. In those cases it is caused by respiratory arrest from failed diaphragm function or cardiac arrest. The brainstem controls spontaneous breathing when one is asleep as it controls maintaining a heartbeat 24 hours a day. You can see that with bulbar polio, if the brainstem cardiac center fails, that the heart will stop beating. As you will find out, in the polio center, breathing will be maintained so respiratory arrest is not possible, but the acute treatment does not prevent cardiac arrest."

Doctor Kelly—"now let's talk about the other 5% of deaths. Complications of a viral infection can be an inflammation of the heart muscle called 'myocarditis.' How this can occur is not yet clear but it can even result from the usually benign 1st degree flu syndrome. An inflamed heart will be diagnosed by abnormal EKG findings which will be discussed during the staff's training program. Suffice to say that an inflamed heart can lead to sudden cardiac arrest or a fatal arrythmia. Myocarditis is often treated as a heart attack with the current meds used in the CCU. And finally, myocarditis often leads to acute and chronic congestive heart failure for which we would begin the standard treatments for CHF."

There was a long pause as Judge Gagnon said, "we are fortunate to be living in our city with a hospital that can treat polio victims, but the city is only less than half of the panhandle's 26 county population.

What happens to the people who live hundreds of miles from Kelly Hospital?"

Doctor Hall looked to Doctor Hallet for an answer. He finally said, "does anyone expect to live with a ruptured abdominal aneurysm? If you live a block away from this hospital, you do. But not if you live a hundred miles away. The reality is that this is your regional hospital. It will provide the state-of-the-art treatment for polio, BUT you, or your family, or friends, or even the lawmen MUST GET YOU HERE. That is the reality we must all live with. To facilitate this, I have sent a letter to all the panhandle's country docs that once they diagnose polio, they need to send the victims directly to the doctor's offices at the Kelly Hospital for an evaluation—and not to delay in case muscle paralysis develops. That is all we can do for people who live far from regional hospital care." After another long pause, Mister Gregory raised his hand.

Mister Gregory—"I gather that polio care can take weeks or months. How is one able to pay for such care?"

Addie said, "finances are my domain. We have applied to UNICEF, the March of Dimes, Federal Health Association, Federal County funds, and will also apply for city subsidies. Other than these associations we will rely on prepaid hospital and medical care programs or private pay from patients. Otherwise, we will be providing much free care. Free care amidst a drought, dust bowl, and a national depression can tax the hospital financial foundation. But we will manage!"

With no further questions, Doctor Hall surprised everyone by saying, "before we move to the polio center and you finally get to see what we do for acute treatment, I would like to do an experiment. Do you all know what it feels like to not be able to take a breath. No, most of us do not know the feeling. So for the next two minutes, I will ask everyone to take a breath and then hold your breath for two minutes till the buzzer sounds off. So take your breath, and on GO, hold your breath. . . GO"

"One minute has passed, keep holding your breath. Some of you are not appearing very comfortable. . .

30 seconds to go and you are all getting air hungry. . . 15 seconds to go and you feel like your brain is about to explode. Hold it. . . hold it. . . and BREATHE."

"Wasn't that awful. . . well polio victims feel just like that before they pass out or die. Suffocation is the worst way to die. Well we have a lifesaving machine to show you. Let's step into the medical ward and we will present the second half of this experience as we guide you thru the breathing center and introduce you to the 'Iron Lung!'"

CHAPTER 3

The Iron Lung

Arriving at the designated spot in the medical ward, the group cautiously entered the breathing center. The two instructor docs saw the unusual facial expression. Jaw dropping 'shock and awe' mixed with apprehension and disbelief. As the entire group entered they encircled nine new pieces of machinery—six tomb like tunnels and three rocking beds. After the appropriate time for all to settle down, Doctor Hall said, "ladies, gentlemen, nurses, and doctors, these are six breathing machines and three recovery beds—the latter which assist breathing by using gravity (more later). We shall now start explaining the breathing machines that are known as the 'iron lung!' We will again provide an introductory presentation and then open the floor for all your questions. To be heard, simply hold a hand up and you'll be recognized in the order we spot you. Doctor Kelly will begin."

1. "This machine, called an iron lung, will breathe for patients who have paralyzed muscles of breathing—the chest intercostals and the diaphragm. This is the acute treatment we have been referring to,"

2. "This miracle invention is made by the Emerson Co. of Cambridge, Massachusetts. The units you see are the updated version."

3. "Basically it is a horizontal cylinder that measures 7 feet long, 2.7 feet wide and over three feet of overhead space."

4. "It weighs 500 pounds and is on wheels for easy maneuverability."

5. "The cover is mostly glass and opens up to expose the entire patient. It is used to perform certain personal tasks. But note the two-minute timer on the top of the dome. It is there to remind workers to complete their tasks or to close the dome and allow the patient to catch

their breath before resuming the needed task. That by the way is not a stock item—we added it for our patients' protection."

6. "The sides each have three sealing portholes used to perform needed tasks. The way they seal will be discussed later."

7. "By releasing these two locking valves, the bed pulls out of the cylinder for easily adding a patient to the machine: or removing the patient during weaning activities. You all need to realize that when a patient is first inserted in the machine all activities are assisted thru the side portholes or the dome is lifted for the two minutes. As the patient starts to recover, the bed is pulled out for patient care and for weaning activities."

8. "When a patient is added to the machine, the only body part that is not in the sealed cylinder is the head. The neck seal is carefully applied to the patient's neck below the voice box. This seal, as well as the six portholes, is made of an elastic spongy rubber that is tightened by

rotating the base in a clockwise fashion till the rubber comfortably seals the neck from the cylinder or seals the six portholes around the attendants' arms."

9. "This brings us to a demonstration. First we will demonstrate the mechanism without a volunteer and then we will add someone to the machine. This machine will breathe by generating a 40-psi negative pressure in the cylinder. When the bellows at the rear of the machine is pulled out, the negative pressure is generated which allows air to enter a patient's lungs as the patient inhales thru the mouth and nose. When the bellow's tension is released, the bellows returns to a neutral position with 0-psi as the patient exhales. Then the cycle resumes. As you can see, the motor is set at 15 respirations per minute—that allows for two seconds to inhale and two seconds to exhale before the four second cycle resumes to get 15 respirations per minute. Humans naturally have 12 respirations per minute which allows a

pause between respirations. But remember we can take a deep breath, but iron lung patients cannot. The volume of air they move in and out is always the same. Now watch as I turn the motor on."

*

One by one, each observer moved along the cylinder to watch the bellows being pulled out as the neck and portholes caved in under the 40-psi of negative pressure. For all 75 participants to see the machine at a closeup took at least a half hour.

Then one of the docs called for a volunteer. Addie had spotted one nurse who always managed to be touching the machine. It was no surprise when Louisa yelled out, "me, I want to go in. This is important to me, heh?" The docs quickly realized the significance of the request and gave their approving nod. The bed was pulled out as Roland, the daytime orderly, offered to lift her into the machine's bed. Once settled in and the neck leather was comfortably applied, the bed was slid into the machine and the motor turned on at 15 respirations per minute. Everyone seemed to be holding their breath as they waited for Louisa's response.

Louisa kept everyone in total suspense for what seemed forever. Suddenly a big smile appeared as Louisa said, "totally amazing. I am not breathing yet the machine is making me breathe. The only difference seems to be the frequent short breaths. This is very comfortable and I can see why paralyzed patients will be happy to be in this machine. I am impressed." As the bed was pulled out, Roland helped Louisa out as Addie realized that there was more to coworkers than met the eye. As Louisa put her feet on the floor she looked at Dottie and whispered, "I want to be one of the nurses assigned to this duty, Ok?" "Yes, we will talk after today's program."

"That does it for our presentation. I am sure that there is so much more to discuss, but we will answer all your questions and if some subjects are not covered we will add a second presentation at the end of the day. So with a show of hands, who is first?"

Mayor. "How long do patients need to go in the machines. Are we talking of hours or days?" "Mayor Monroe, we are talking of weeks or months." After a loud gasp from the group, Doc Hall continued. "The 2nd degree victims with mild to moderate paralysis of arms, legs, and intercostal breathing muscles will spend an average of two solid weeks in the iron lung. Then we will start the weaning process which will take at least two weeks till we can move the patient to the rocking beds during the daytime but return to the iron lung for bedtime. During another two weeks in the rocking bed, the patient's muscle strength weakens from working all day and must rest at night in the iron lung. Now for the more severe 2nd degree every timeframe is doubled or tripled—yes it is not unusual for severe 2nd degree cases to continuously be in the iron lung for six weeks plus six weeks of weaning and six more weeks on the rocking bed."

Council lady. "Can we stop and explain how the rocking bed works?" "Sure, a patient is laying flat on their back. When the motor starts, the head of the bed goes up 45 degrees. This pulls the diaphragm downward by gravity and the air enters the lungs. When the head of bed goes flat or beyond, the diaphragm relaxes and the patient can exhale. You do realize that it is the patient who is initiating the respiration but it is gravity that cuts down the work of breathing. Yet at the end of a set number of hours, the patient wears out and is happy to return to the iron lung. Day by day we increase the number of weaning hours till they can spend all day in the rocking bed." The council lady added, "how do you decide when a patient is ready for the rocking bed?" At two weeks or less, we watch what the patient can do when the motor is off and the dome is open. It is a slow process but when a patient can comfortably breathe spontaneously for five minutes without turning blue, we continue the weaning process to get the patient to spend an hour in the rocking bed where the weaning process continues. But remember, their time in the rocking bed is during the daytime as bedtime is spent back in the iron lung in case the musculature weakens during sleep when the patient could die of hypoxia or CO_2 narcosis and acidosis."

Louisa. Instead of being back in the iron lung at night, couldn't oxygen supplementation be used to prevent hypoxia?" "Yes hypoxia can be prevented, but if the patient is not properly breathing, CO_2 will accumulate and lead to CO_2 narcosis where the blood becomes acidic, the patient goes into coma, and dies of a cardiac arrest despite having a good blood oxygen level."

Another nurse. "If a patient spends two weeks on his back, decubitus skin ulcers (bed sores) will appear. What do you do to prevent this?" "Good skin care to include heat treatments, massage, bathing, creams, and so on. Plus these two knobs will turn the bed right or left to get the patient off his back. But note, the bed does not turn either way more than 45 degrees. With a patient on his 90-degree side, the negative pressure breathing will only inflate the top lung properly and the bottom lung will not because of the body's weight on the bottom chest wall. Cycling this 45-degree position is very important for patient comfort and preventing skin pressure ulcers. Before I forget, patients cannot be placed on their abdomen since the body's weight will prevent the chest cavity from expanding."

Mister Gregrory. "Not to get off the subject, but I am stuck on statistics. You said that the panhandle will likely get a minimum of 32 paralyzed cases per 100,000. Yet you also could get up to five times that number.

Now with the Kelly Hospital being the regional hospital, you will get all the cases to treat—but you have only six iron lungs and three rocking beds. How can you expect to handle a sudden influx of more paralyzed patients when you already have a full house?" "We have planned for this. First of all, paralyzed patients appear in spurts of isolated events—or intermittent epidemics. We are not likely going to receive more than one to three at a time. But not denying that the worst could happen, we can get as many iron lungs from the state bank in Dallas which is controlled by the Dallas Medical Center where we all trained. With the telegraph, we can get an emergency delivery within 8 hours on the daytime train and 6 hours from the overnight express. Plus let us not forget that the medical ward will have some acute cases that are being observed. Now that gives us time to make allowances since a patient with polio doesn't stop breathing in a matter of one breath to total respiratory arrest on the next breath, it is a gradual one even if sometimes it is faster than anticipated."

Principal MacBride. "The death rate confuses me. You said that 2-5 percent of kids will die from this infection as the adult rate can vary between 5 and 30%. With the schedule you presented as the acute treatment and the strict safe weaning protocol, there has to be another cause for the death rate?" "Yes, unfortunately the death rate from polio is based on the four degrees of involvement we initially described. It is easy to see that the 4th degree patients are not expected to survive and the severely affected bulbar polio is also in the same category when the brainstem center for heartbeat maintenance is destroyed. Yet even when we are dealing with the mild to moderate to severe 2nd degree, some patients still do not survive.

The cause is associated complications of which myocarditis is the most common." "Which is?"

"When the polio virus causes fever in the early stage, it means that the virus is in the bloodstream. The virus can cause an inflammation of the heart muscle that is called myocarditis. Inflamed heart muscles cause all sorts of bad arrythmias of which the dreaded ventricular tachycardia that progresses to ventricular fibrillation with seizures, and then death. We will be treating the documented cases of myocarditis with the advanced drugs we use in the CCU. Despite their use, myocarditis is one of the major causes of long-term congestive heart failure if one is lucky enough to survive the initial insult."

Another nurse, "How do you know if a patient has myocarditis since there are very few symptoms especially in children?" "We might have mentioned this in our polio discussion, but all patients going into an iron lung have a baseline chest Xray, EKG, CBC, electrolytes, blood sugar, and one liver/kidney function blood test. Myocarditis causes all sorts of EKG findings to include: prolongation of the Q-T interval, widening of QRS complex, ST elevation, bradycardia, heart block, tachycardia, and pvcs just to name a few. The chest Xray might show cardiomegaly (an enlarged heart) or even congestive heart failure."

Head nurse Scanlon. "Getting back to patient care, how do these patients feed?" "Just like you and I except that an attendant has to place food morsels in their mouths. After chewing, the patient swallows during the exhalation phase. OF note is that swallowing muscles can be affected with bulbar polio." "How about bathing?" "It can be done thru the portholes over a prolonged period of time. But our experience is to let four nurses open the dome and you would be surprised to see the entire body soaped, scrubbed, rinsed, and dried under two minutes." "Any others that come to mind?" "Toileting is by far the most dreaded by patients and staff. Yet, once you get by the embarrassment, it becomes just another job that total patient care demands. Others include inserting and maintaining catheters, menstrual flow care, massaging painful muscles, IV maintenance for dehydrated patients, even down to scratching every inch of a human's body. Total care is just that, these patients cannot do a thing for themselves except to feel useless and humiliated. Thus the biggest nursing responsibility is to maintain a patient's morale, wellbeing, and motivation to get better. There will be more nursing training once we establish a group of selected workers in the polio breathing center."

Sheriff Butler. "Hate to go back, but I could not get your attention. Back to sudden death, are you planning to perform CPR?" "Yes and No. Let me explain. It goes without saying that Doctor Hall and I will go to extreme lengths to save a child's life. If that means extensive CPR, then so be it. Now when it comes to adults it all depends on age, degree of paralysis, concurrent other medical conditions, and the most important, the patients' directives. As you can see it is a multifactorial situation that we hope to settle early in the patient's illness."

Another nurse. "You said that oxygen was not given to patients while in the Iron Lung. What about the oxygen we empirically give to our heart attack victims.

Does that include the myocarditis and CHF groups?" "Yes those patients definitely will benefit being on supplemental oxygen because of the presumed benefit to myocarditis and CHF patients."

The council lady. "As a non-medical person, how do you determine if a polio victim under observation is losing breathing muscle strength and now belongs in an 'Iron lung?" "We could just ask the patients if they feel air hunger, if they are tiring, or they have peripheral cyanosis seen under the fingernails. But we follow a more objective method. There is a simple machine made up of a graduated glass tube attached to a mouthpiece. An adult's normal breathing volume is 500 ml and a 50-pound child is about 250 ml. If the measured volume is only at 50%, then it is time to move the patient to an iron lung. Another way of testing a patient's breathing potential is to measure their forced tidal volume of forced inspired air. Adults can reach 3000 ml as kids are more in the 1500 ml range. This simple machine is called a spirometer and one will be placed in each doctor's office, several in the observation medical ward, and one for each iron lung." A spirometer was shown to the crowd as Doctor Hall demonstrated the rising ball to a nice even breathing volume of 500 ml in and out, and then a demonstrated forced breathing volume to a max tidal volume of 2,800 ml. PS, by the way, the iron lung negative pressure of 40 psi will generate an adult tidal volume of +- 500 ml and a child's psi setting is set according to a chart based on body weight."

Another councilman. "It seems to me that a lot of this fenagling to decide when to use an iron lung could be avoided by simply measuring a patient's blood oxygen level just like you measure a blood sugar level? "Yes that is true, but unlike measuring blood sugar, we do not have the technology to measure a patient's blood oxygen level. And when we ever get the technology, it will require an arterial sample and not the easy current methods of vein blood sampling."

Louisa was mesmerized by the equipment and finally said, "why a mirror and a metal frame above the patient's face?" "The frame is to hold a book, magazine, or newspaper. The only problem is that someone has to turn the pages, which is where family, friends, or volunteers can help. The mirror is to give the patient an ability to look around, talk to a neighbor, watch the nurses do their work but again someone needs to move the mirror around to provide the views."

Addie. "What is the downside to paralyzed muscles?" "Unattended paralyzed muscles can lead to disabling permanent contractures. To avoid this is passive exercises and aggressive deep muscle massage. This can be done by a professional physical therapist who can do the treatment and even train the nurses to continue the exercises whenever they are free of other duties. For your information, we now have two certified physical therapists on staff who will treat the patients and train the nurses. As a matter of fact, volunteers can also be trained to do the job. Plus this work starts thru the portholes when the patient is in the iron lung."

Mayor Monroe. "Although I am following you, I keep thinking of the 5-30% death rate you quoted. That worries me." "First of all, that is the death rate for all four degrees of polio involvement. Now if you take the 2nd degree we realize that this will likely be 90 % of the patients we will be treating. Out of this class +- 98 % will be going home with or without residual. Now I know you wonder why any could die, well myocarditis and CHF can occur in any degree of involvement even the 1st degree which is supposed to be a minor flu syndrome—as mentioned that fever and viremia are not preventable and often lead to carditis. We cannot prevent these complications, and have very little we can do to treat them."

Addie. "So treatment of 2nd degree with residual symptoms will need care after discharge. To what degree?" "Any polio victim with residual symptoms will need aggressive physical therapy. Some of the exercises can be done at home, but the best treatment is to use multiple machines that do the proper work under resistance. That means, an outpatient treatment center monitored by a physical therapist, with the modern machines to do the work." "I see, so that means an allotment of space to set up a post discharge treatment center with machines to purchase?" "Yes, but look at the bright side, the inpatients will be using the machinery and outpatient services are billed separately from the hospital expenses."

Louisa. "Are paralyzed muscles painful and what can be done about it?" "Yes, these muscles are a source of steady pain made worse with cramps. There is a standard treatment called 'Kenny' hot moist packs that cut down cramping and help relieve pain. If not effective, the docs can give an intramuscular injection of 'intocostrin' which is a muscle relaxant derived from curare. The hot packs generally work but are time consuming for the nurses and volunteers would again help in preparing and applying the packs."

Another councilman. "You said that patients in an iron lung can talk. Is that universal?" "For 2nd degree patients, yes. But don't forget we will get some patients with 3rd degree bulbar paralysis. These patients are at risk of losing speech, swallowing, ocular movements, and getting ptosis (drooping eyelids). When these functions fail, the brainstem is severely affected and the prognosis is very grave. Need I say more?"

Mister Gregory. "So what happens when the power goes off?" "The hospital is completely electrified and air conditioned. That was costly and we have not been able to finance a generator. So without power it is a matter of 'drop what you are doing' and RUN to the polio center to help operating the iron lung manually. Watch Doc Kelly." "You disengage the motor/transmission and pull the top lever down till the negative pressure goes up to 40 psi as the leather bellows is pulled out; then let it go to allow exhalation at a rate of 15 respirations per minute. That can quickly be tiring so you add your foot to the foot pedal and use it in conjunction with the top handle." After a demonstration, Mister Gregory added, "I see, but what do you do if the power is out for a day or so?" "Then we call our volunteer list and use them. Generally, one hour is just about what most operators can last. Some last longer by breaking it up into half hour sessions."

Mayor Monroe. "I hate to admit my ignorance, but is this polio a new epidemic and is it limited to the United States?" "Polio has been around for 2000 years and is documented in the written word since the time of Jesus Christ. Today it is a worldwide problem where the death rate is very high in developing third world countries because they cannot afford an Emerson Iron Lung. Fortunately, the Australian President has converted his automobile manufacturing factory and is building iron lungs out of plywood and is giving them all over to the third world countries."

Mister True, RR manager. "As an outsider, I have two questions. First, is who maintains these machines?" "Today, we have hired a local mechanic to do the weekly maintenance. The word is that the March of Dimes will eventually take over. For now, the expense is ours." "Secondly, when I came here months ago I was told that I was coming to a community with a top-notch hospital and that is why I have prepaid health insurance with Kelly Hospital. To get to the point, it is clear you have complete control of the oncoming epidemic as the panhandle and this city will be well served, but I think you are shortchanging yourselves. You need to prepare for cases coming in from New Mexico, Colorado, and Oklahoma. And with enough said I refer to Mister Gregrory who planted the idea in my head."

Addie looked surprised and finally said, "well Mister Gregory what is meant by Mister True's insinuations?" "Well it is complicated and I think we should discuss this in private." Taking the hint, she then said, "that does it for this presentation, if any of you would care to join us as medical caregivers or as volunteers, please stay for a brief discussion. Thank you for attending and wish us well with our undertaking."

Left in the breathing center were Louisa, Roland, the lady councilman, Minister Tillotson, one evening nurse, two nightshift nurses and all the doctors and their wives. Addie then said, "thank you for finding the calling to help these dependent victims. Eventually everyone will be given an assignment after we accumulate a full working staff. However, we cannot accept the obstetric and nursery staff for fear of transmitting the virus to mothers and babies."

*

With everyone gone, the Duo and the new Quad met in private with Mister Gregory. Brad started by saying, "well Sir, kindly explain what Mister True was insinuating." "Well I don't like being the devil's advocate, but this is very important. Addie and Brad, you don't realize the respect that Kelly Hospital has gained since you opened your doors 25 years ago. The fact that you have been performing specialized surgical procedures, you have already enhanced the respect that people feel towards you all. There is no doubt in my mind that all docs from here to Albuquerque, NM, from here to Pueblo, Co, and from here to Oklahoma City, will send their polio patients to Amarillo for specialty care. The result will turn your regional hospital into a tertiary medical center like Dallas is for points south. Amarillo will become the catchment area for points east, west, and north." There was a pause as no one dared speak.

Gregory continued. "Let's do a reality check. The next ten years will be troubled times for any business including a private hospital. The national depression will persist but hopefully will turn around over many years starting with the next election in 1932. We are in a drought and the panhandle's high plains have become a dust bowl. The people will have to leave to survive. To get to the 40's, will be a challenge and even with your determination, your hospital, like many others, could fail!"

"The reality is that there may not be many referrals for specialized surgeries. Only the very ill will appear in the ER for medical or surgical emergency care. The only advancing medical dilemma is the growing epidemic of paralyzing polio. So the issue is not just about surviving but this polio scourge is an opportunity to thrive just like you did during the 1918 Influenza pandemic. Thriving because you can give expert state-of-the-art care is not a predatory practice, it is staying with the times that modern science provides."

Addie added, "assuming you are correct, and we have no basis to contradict you, what do you recommend we should do to prepare. Turn this hospital into the NTPTC—or the Northern Texas Polio Treatment Center and boldly advertise it in every newspaper from here to Albuquerque, Pueblo, and Oklahoma City." "To make this happen, what do you propose we change to make ready?" "I am proposing a major overhaul to include the following:

1. Move the current post-op surgical ward to the specialized surgical ward next to the current operating room suites and recovery room. Without many referrals, the few surgical cases that come thru the ER will fill the current empty surgical post-op rooms.

2. Renovate the old original surgical ward. As you enter the ward, convert several rooms to make an outpatient physical therapy center for continuing care. The advantage is that the recovering inpatients will also use the

exercise machinery that will be housed in the center.

3. The next portion of the new ward will include the unchanged double rooms of patients under observation for signs of respiratory failure.

4. The next and last portion of the ward will be a wide-open breathing center of at least a dozen 'iron lungs' and six rocking beds. This is the heart of the treatment center. It will include three physician offices, a large nurses' station/private area, a volunteer office, a pharmacy, a smaller charge nurse's office, a physical therapy office, a refrigerated unit to hold snacks between meals, a utility room for personal care materials, a room to prepare hot packs, and a large storage area for the extra iron lungs and rocking beds.

5. Build a nursing staff willing to work with such patients. Do not hesitate to pay higher wages for what is often referred to as 'combat pay.' There is no doubt these workers will be working themselves to physical and mental

exhaustion after a full shift. Put all workers thru a rigorous training program and do not minimize the care these victims will need.

6. Then advertise in all our newspapers for volunteers to assist the nursing and physical therapy staff in caring for these dependent cases. Be forthcoming and include the jobs that volunteers can do such as bathing, toileting, feeding, reading, muscle massage, ROM (range of motion) exercises, and Kenny hot packs for muscle cramps. Always finish each ad with the statement, 'if the next victim is a family member, we will be here to care for them.'

7. Set up an on-call volunteer list for those who prefer to work when there is an extra need.

8. Spend the money and purchase a 50 Amp generator that can operate some twenty combined iron lungs and rocking beds as well as the lighting to keep the breathing center operational.

9. Hire enough physical therapists to care for twelve iron lungs and the many patients in the outpatient center.

10. Add the two other medical doctors to join the polio center.

11. Use surgeons. First, they are true medical doctors before becoming surgeons. Some will be used to add abdominal feeding tubes, perform tracheostomies, or give muscle cramp injections. But all can be used to work in the physical therapy outpatient department. They can also evaluate new cases and operate the spirometers to help them decide if someone needs an admission for observation.

12. Last of all, order another nine iron lungs and seven rocking beds to be fully prepared to fill the breathing center and storage of extra units."

Brad was stunned as he said, "wow, that is a major undertaking without any guarantees that Amarillo and outlying communities will be affected as predicted." Addie added, "were we to get bold and plan on being a tertiary treatment center, we would have to start the renovation right away to be prepared—for if you advertise then it implies that you are ready to receive patients! The problem is money. We have a guarded medical fund geared to keeping this hospital open for years to come despite the national depression and local drought. We cannot touch this fund as a matter of principle. So where do we get the money to pay for all this?"

There was another long pause as Mister Gregory finally said, "it was wise to apply to the UNICEF, March of Dimes, County coffers, and Federal Health but I do not think you will get a penny from them for such a small center compared to the large centers especially in the east. So go with the following:

1. Apply in person to the city council. I will be there to push the members on their generosity's weakest link! It is their responsibility to support the health of the taxpayers.

2. Although the local Wells Fargo branch is stressed to the maximum, let us not forget

that Wells Fargo was heavily invested in railroads. Not being part of the stock market, and subsidized by the Feds, they are still in the business of lending money to solid customers. There is no doubt that Kelly Hospital is in that favorable category. With a mortgage free hospital you have collateral as real-estate with value for the buildings and land. Besides the bank has to do its share in supporting the local hospital and medical care. Oh, and let's not forget that I am on the bank's Board of Trustees that approves loans, heh?

3. Last of all, you know I will support you 100%. If all fails, I will be your sugar daddy. As far as I am concerned, this hospital has performed miracles and it deserves to stay open at all costs. On a personal level, let it be said that I will cover any expenses that is not covered by the Polio Center's income. This is a gift to you and not a loan, for, besides predicting that you will thrive, I cannot live with the idea

of anyone suffocating to death. So accept my donation of $5,000 and get Mike Walters to start the renovations ASAP."

**

CHAPTER 4

Building the Polio Center

That night, the Duo was having an emergency meeting in their hot bathtub. Brad started, "boy what a day. The second presentation with the day nurses, ancillary workers, and invited local merchants was an active one to say the least." "Did you notice how Doctor Hallet was very quiet?" "Yes but he often smiled and nearly busted open when Mister Gregory suggested we could become a tertiary medical center in the care of polio victims!" "Yes and after the meeting he confirmed that this would likely happen with our good caring record. He even volunteered to notify all the doctors in the 26 panhandle counties of our plans." "Great, that is one thing we won't have to do, heh? And by the way, I have decided to put surgery on hold and work with you to operate this treatment center." Glad to have you; then let's talk about the coming work we need to do."

"First, did you ever get the name of that volunteering councilwoman?" "Yes, it is Marylyn Dudley and I offered her the department head position. She accepted and would also be a working department head." "Great, now how many nurses did we get to work in the new center?" "Ten nurses and two orderlies." "Lastly, how much should we offer the staff that is willing to move to the breathing center, or observation rooms, or even the rehab center?" "I have thought about it, discussed it with Dottie and Susie, and because the breathing center is such a high stress and emotional environment, I think we should offer time-and-a-half for anyone working in the breathing center and regular pay for those working in the observation and rehab departments." "Ok!"

Addie hesitated and came back with, "what do you think of Louisa?" "Other than the fact she is cute, weighs 80 pounds and is only 4'11" inches tall. Well let me tell you she looked like an angel in that iron lung and just about got all the merchants to start sniffing to hide their wet eyes. Besides that, I know what you meant. Well she has the energy and shows a real interest in paralyzed patients. I think she should be the head of the department!" "Agree, but what does Dottie and Susie say about that?" "They are the ones who suggested her name right from the start." "Ok!"

"Out of curiosity, how many volunteers did we get from the presentation?" "As of today, we have Marylyn, Minister Tillotson and his wife, four merchant wives, and two councilman's wives for a total of nine. Plus, I will start advertising in the local papers as early as tomorrow since, along with Dottie and Susie, we need to design a training program for them as well as the nursing staff." "As far as volunteers to assist nurses, who else do we need?" "A strong man and replacements for every shift, an orderly for every shift, and at least a fulltime mechanic to service the machines."

"Did we get any donations other than Mister Gregory's $5,000?" "Yes, after Louisa's exposition, you could tell that the merchants were affected. After the presentation six came forward and each donated $500." "And what did you give them in return?" "I gave them an 8-inch bright red predrilled heart plaque with the saying in white letters, 'We support our Polio Center.'" "Good move and if that doesn't bring in more donations, then nothing will. Speaking of donations, are we still planning to request a subsidy from the mayor and city council?" "Absolutely, I thought we should schedule if for a week from now to give the members ample time to think about it." "Ok!"

Brad was ready to get out of the tub as he added, "well we had a heck of a day with two presentations, gaining several working staff to switch to the polio center, signing up volunteers, getting $8,000 in donations, and finding our new head nurse and head volunteer. Now thanks to Mister Gregory we are expanding, renovating, and doubling our polio center. In the morning we will be transferring post-op patients to the specialized post-op ward and in the afternoon we'll be going over the renovations with

Mike and emptying the patient rooms that will become part of the rehab and breathing center. Guess it is a go, heh?" Without thinking Brad got up and said, "this has been a long meeting and my fingers and toes are getting prune-ish. Time to get out and dry out." Addie started laughing as she said, "yes, and your tilly-wacker tip is also turning into a prune. Besides all this, I have some bad news. We completely missed a crucial issue in the management of polio victims going home with residual symptoms. As Dottie and Susie pointed out, these patients will need canes or crutches, but also short and long-term durable braces or wheelchairs!" "Oh my, that sounds like another extended discussion, so let's get dressed and we'll continue this in our parlor with a fresh cup of coffee as we let the prunes plump back up, heh?"

*

The story started as Addie said, "we have one physical therapist who has worked well taking care of fractures and specialized orthopedic procedures. With the impending polio epidemic, he is planning to get involved with the polio victims but one therapist is not enough. Mister Gregory suggested we needed four but the girls (Dottie and Susie) feel we need three as long as one is also doubly certified in physical therapy and orthotics." "Whoa and what is an orthotist?"

"To explain, let's step back a bit. We have a democrat planning to run for office in the coming election. His name is Franklin Delano Roosevelt. Some 30 years ago he had polio and still uses a wheelchair or a long leg brace called a KAFO (knee-ankle-foot orthosis). This brace is secured with a leather cuff above the ankle and at mid-thigh. It also has a knee hinge that permits knee flexion during gait and locking in full extension with a heel strike. This allows standing erect for prolonged periods of time. The brace starts below the foot and extends upward behind the calf and ends in mid-thigh. There are many other braces for the legs and similar ones for the arms. Plus there are some crucial braces to prevent scoliosis from unevenly affected paraspinal muscles."

"So to answer your question, an orthotist is a trained physical therapist who measures patients for the many different braces available for legs, arms, and spines. He can also repair the braces and do minor adjustments for a proper comfortable fit. For more information on this subject, we'll need to ask the girls or an orthotist we hire—especially the back braces to control scoliosis, heh?" "For sure!"

"So in the AM we'll do the patient transfers and empty the rooms that will be converted into a rehab center and a breathing center. After lunch we'll meet with Mike and then start advertising locally for volunteers as well as physical therapists at the large hospitals in Dallas, Albuquerque, and Oklahoma City." "Yep, the only thing remaining is my deep protein injection that will settle my nerves—for all this talk of renovations and a new center is raising hell with my sleep!"

*

The cafeteria was full of volunteers who had gathered for a free breakfast and a half a day of work. Their jobs were to wheel the patients from one ward to another and transfer the beds and other room furniture to their new rooms or to the large storage area next to the outpatient rehab waiting room. At 8AM sharp, the post-op head nurse started the transfer and managed the traffic to avoid a jam. By 10AM the patients were well situated in private rooms located in their new post-op surgical ward. For the next two hours, three rooms were emptied for the rehab center, two for orthotics storage, two for the waiting room and one for more storage. That left 10 rooms on either side of the ward. Four rooms on each side of the hall were needed for the new breathing center and one room on each side was used for storing the extra iron lungs, rocking beds, and individual cots for close family members: so that left rooms on each side of the hall for observation. By noon the volunteers were given a free hot lunch and thanked for their work.

As expected, Mike showed up for lunch. The small talk progressed to more of a business aspect. Addie then said, "the reason you are here is because we want to build a new polio center out of the original surgical ward. The present center consists of a breathing center in the medical ward where we did not need to do any renovations since we used the actual old ward for multiple patients. Now we know we will need more room and so we have emptied the old surgical ward and will ask you to renovate it into three separate departments. The first, a rehab center with an orthotics storage and fitting room, a waiting room and public bathrooms. The second is for patient observation rooms, and the third is for the actual breathing center—plus all three will need a nurses' counter."

Mike had been listening and finally said, "The actual job to do the carpentry work is not a problem since my six men are laid off. We shall not have a problem finding electricians and plumbers as well as the local supplies they need. What will be difficult is to order certain items that are not available in local stores. But for now, let's get started on a detailed tour so I have a better idea of what will be needed."

The Duo stood by Mike at the old entrance to the surgical ward. "Standing here, build a doorless archway with a sign overhead that reads, 'Kelly

Hospital Polio Center.'" "On the right is a gutted three-room unit that will be our rehab center. Build an entrance door and a sign overhead that reads 'Rehab Center.' Leave one bathroom. The next two gutted rooms are to be the orthotics' room for braces. Run a series of hooks five feet off the floor on one wall, shelves on another, and on the short wall add a 6-foot-long padded patient table that is 36 inches high. Leave the bathroom." "What about the rehab center?" "For now leave it open till we get the exercise machinery and decide what we need for shelving and or other cabinets." "Done!"

"On the left are two gutted rooms that needs to be turned into a one room waiting area with an open archway and a sign over head that reads 'Rehab Waiting Room.' Also add a double public bathroom. The next gutted room is for more storage so leave the single bathroom." "Done!"

"So that now brings us some three rooms down the hallway. Here is where you put the first steel insulated double doors with a sign overhead that reads, 'Polio Observation Rooms—walk thru to the

Breathing Center.' Just inside the double doors you add a counter type nurses station where the head nurse can direct visitors. You then walk right through the observation rooms to this point. Here you place the second steel insulated double doors with a sign overhead that reads, 'The Breathing Polio Center— please be quiet and only one visitor at a time.'"

"Done!"

Standing by the entrance door, Brad said, "remove the partition walls between the four far rooms on the right and left. Leave one bathroom on each side, add ceiling lights with individual wall switches, and ten surface outlets on the near, the far wall, and an extra five on the outside connecting wall—all wires covered in hard conduits. Leave the fifth room untouched for storing the extra iron lungs, rocking beds, family cots, and leave the bathroom as is. In addition leave the present nurses' nurses' station, nurses' changing and bathrooms, pharmacy, and doctors' offices in place. Four your info, this large open room will house twelve iron lungs, six rocking beds, and two single bathrooms for public use. Plus each iron lung needs three chairs—one for the nurse, the family member, and the volunteer or orderly." "Done, but where do the other family members, who are waiting to take their turns, sit?" "In the rehab waiting room where they can visit and raise all sorts of noise. When the visiting family member leaves, they can escort the second family member to enter the breathing center." "Got it!"

With the tour finished, the group walked back to the cafeteria to discuss the renovation specifics. Brad then asked, "so what do you perceive might be problems in doing the renovations?" "The carpentry aspect of removing partition walls and bathrooms is fairly straight forward except that we need to be careful in removing electrical wires, oxygen lines, outlets, and wall switches. Any new outlet and switches will need to be surface wiring inside hard conduits. In addition, the extra lighting will also be surface mounts but the wiring for them will be in the ceiling space and will not show. As far as parts, I am certain that we will find everything in local stores and lumber yards." "So what is the hitch to get the project completed in a timely fashion."

"The only problem will be those insulated steel double doors before the observation rooms and the breathing center. Those will come from Houston and if they are not in their warehouse, no one knows when they will arrive. So this is what I can offer you. We can do this project in seven to ten days without waiting for steel doors. To maintain the privacy you want, we would install pre-fabricated wooden doors that will work till the steel doors arrive."

Addie added, "so when can you start?" "This afternoon, I have electricians and plumbers waiting as we speak. They need to stay ahead of us to deactivate electricity and water lines before we tear down the walls."

Addie then asked, "what will this cost us?" Those steel insulated doors will cost $125 each and will need payment up front. The chairs you need will be available at the furniture store and we can take care of that. The remainder of the work is all labor plus miscellaneous supplies. We can wait to tabulate the hours and supplies once the project is done." Addie then gave him a $1,000 bank draft to order the steel doors, the chairs, and make payroll for the workers.

*

The next day, the Duo planned each day during the morning breakfast till they reached their estimated 7-10-day goal.

DAY ONE. Brad was supervising the removal of all partition walls while saving doors, outlets, and ceiling light switches. The plumbers were removing wash sinks and toilets while capping the pipes and sewer lines. Amidst all that, the electricians were still working on the electrical systems in the overhead spaces. In short it was a day of controlled demolition and hauling away the piles of useless lumber, sheetrock, and old knob and tube wiring in the partition walls. Some of the finish carpenters were covering the plumbing in removed bathrooms with on site fabricated cabinets that hid water and sewage lines.

Addie was busy at the telegraph office and the local newspapers. At the newspapers she prepared an ad requesting a mechanic to maintain the respiratory equipment and for volunteers to help the staff caring for paralyzed polio victims. Afterwards she composed a long telegraph letter to the four bordering medical centers—Dallas, Albuquerque, Oklahoma City, and Pueblo. Each of those letters were sent to the medical education office care of the center's director. The letter clearly stated that the Kelly Hospital Polio Treatment Center was in need of two certified physical therapists and one orthotist—ASAP.

At the end of the day, Addie posted a signup sheet in the cafeteria for all shifts during weekday and weekends. The advertised pay rate was time-and-a-half for all breathing center workers—but the pay raise excluded nurses in the observation and rehab centers. Although these nurses would receive standard pay per shift, at least they would be working and not be on the laid off group without pay.

Since many nurses were in the laid off group, the nursing director's staff was calling them and informing them of the sign-up sheet in the cafeteria. At lunch time, Louisa was standing by the sign-up sheet and was answering questions. At the end of the lunch break, the sign-up sheet was full. Some working nurses made a lateral move in hopes of maintaining continuous employment, but the bulk of the nursing staff came from the laid off group.

DAY TWO. Addie was on the phone with the Houston distribution center to order nine more iron lungs and three more rocking beds. To her surprise only rocking beds were available. The dispatch officer pointed out that California was flooded with polio cases from China and the Philippines. They were getting all the machines that were available west of the Mississippi. Keeping the Kelly Hospital on top of the waiting list, Addie was sent a set of blueprints for making iron lungs out of plywood.

When the blueprints arrived, Brad spent a long time checking them out. He then walked to see Mike who said that his special woodshop could easily build one. For the rest of the day, Brad worked with the woodshop and ran about town to pick-up the hardware to include hinges, wheels, bellows, leather porthole closures, safety glass, motor and transmission, and pedal hardware for manual operation.

That same day, the girls were busy setting up a training program for the nursing staff and the volunteers. Concurrently, Addie was signing up local volunteers that seemed to match the personalities of the nursing staff and the original volunteers from the first educational presentation.

DAY THREE. Mike finished the demolition and started the 'finish' work. First they had to repair the damaged floor tiles, then they started laying surface conduits for the new insulated wires that had all three pvc coated white negative, a black positive, and green ground.

The Duo interviewed the only applicant for the mechanic's job. Roger Messier was a soft-spoken man, married with three kids and just 40 years old. Since the market crash his hours had been cut down to six hours a day. Finishing at 3PM, he pointed out that he could come to the hospital and service one machine each day while working in the adjacent storage room. The conversation was easily maintained and after a half hour he was hired to do two hours of work each day—while bringing his tools, grease, and oils.

That same day, the girls and Louisa were conducting their training classes for nurses and orderlies. Three, four-hour classes, of 10 staff members produced a full workday.

DAY FOUR. The girls and Louisa trained the growing number of 30 local volunteers on how to help nurses by following their direction and learn some basic skills in hygiene and toileting. Mike was busy setting up new ceiling lights and all the outlets and switches needed. Brad spent the day working with the master carpenters building their first wooden iron lung. Addie was checking statistics of polio cases all over California as well as Seattle, Cheyenne, Chicago, Indiana, and Tennessee. There was no doubt that the virus was headed to northern Texas.

DAY FIVE. Addie was busy picking up sheets, blankets, buttoned-up pajamas, pillows, and several other personal items. Everything was placed in the new cabinets by Louisa. Mike was finishing the breathing center as the finish carpenters and electricians were closing the rehab center and waiting room. By 1PM, the six original iron lungs and three rocking beds were moved into the new breathing center.

DAY SIX. The Duo and the girls were heading to the weekly council meeting. Entering the mayor's meeting room the medical team was introduced to the two new council members as Marylyn and Mister Gregory were well known. Brad and Addie knew the new members Aloysius Talbot, owner of the shoe factory, and Ben Moriarity, major cattleman in the area. Both men were money hungry successful businessmen and would be a major opposition for subsidizing the Polio Center. The invited guest was Mister True representing the railroad. Brad started the meeting.

"Well history repeats itself, "when we built the hospital, you offered us money which we did not need or take, With the 1918 Influenza, we asked for a subsidy but were denied because there was yet any signs of the scourge. After months of intensive disease and our saving ward, we came back and you finally offered us some funds to defray some of our expenses—after the fact, heh? So here we are, there is another epidemic coming our way so do we get a subsidy before or after the epidemic." Addie added, "it would be nice if history did not repeat itself, heh?"

There was a long pause as the mayor stated. "I am sure you realize that the city coffers are very low. With the stock market failure and the depression, people are not able to pay their taxes and everyone is in arears." There was another long pause as Mister Talbot added, "plus we are not certain that we'll even get polio cases, so to subsidize without proof of cause is a bit off a good business move."

Addie jumped off and said, "we are surrounded by polio cases in California, Seattle, Cheyenne, Chicago, Indiana, and Tennessee. It is just a matter of time for northern Texas to be hit both locally, from our panhandle counties, and even from outlying countryside in New Mexico, Colorado, and Oklahoma. To not believe the epidemic is only days away is downright dumb, stupid, and brainless!"

Marylyn and Mister Gregory were relieved to hear the facts. The two new councilmen were huffing away and insisted on a retraction. Mayor Monroe finally jumped in and asked, "how much has it cost you to get ready for this epidemic?" Addie said, "$9,000 from the first order of iron lungs and rocking beds, $9,000 from the second order of the same, and $5,000 for renovations." "And did you take a bank loan?" "No we paid cash out of our personal funds—not the hospital fund."

Councilman Moriaty added, "well that makes it sound like a personal investment in the hopes of making a profit. We do not get involved in speculative investments, there is no way we would subsidize your venture."

After a long pause, Brad stood up and said, "our taxes for the coming year are $6,225. As of this moment, we are applying for a nonprofit status and that means that we will be free of local property taxes or federal income taxes. That is how we treat hostile councils and it will get worse. God forbid you do not experience a catastrophic event like a train derailment or the like and expect your hostile hospital to save your precious paying customers. Make arrangements with your nearest medical center in Dallas—for they are only 300 miles away, heh?"

Addie added, "gentlemen, we did not come here to beg for money. Knowing our expenses should be enough to get a local subsidy. If that fails, then we are leaving." As the medical team got up to leave, Mister Gregory spoke up. "I am ashamed of all of you. That is not how you treat our medical personnel. These are our doctors and our hospital. Think about what you are doing and tell me where you will bring your paralyzed loved ones when they get polio and cannot breathe. Addie was right, you are idiots and I am resigning from this stupid and brainless council." Marylyn got up and added, "and so do I. I cannot work with money hungry ungrateful arrogance."

DAY SEVEN. To everyone's surprise the two insulated double doors arrived as the carpenters were busy installing them. There was no sign of a generator yet.

That same day, a 7-year-old boy came to the office complaining of leg pain as the parents were afraid it was polio. Dottie suspected a hip problem and took X Rays. The diagnosis was Legg-Perthes disease—a vascular insufficiency to the femoral head leading to bony disintegration. Since treatment was not clear, the boy was admitted to the medical ward for further evaluation and treatment.

DAY EIGHT. The Duo and the Quad were having breakfast as two strangers appeared at the ordering counter. No one was impressed till the couple turned around with a cup of coffee and a pastry. The Quad was up and hugging the two strangers. Susie looked at the gal and said, "what is this on your finger?" The lady said, "well since you left I met the man of my dreams, got engaged, graduated, and then got married. Now we are both looking for a job and Doctor Huxley sent us here. We are applying for three jobs—two physical therapy jobs and one orthotist job. Yes, this is my hubby, Abe Strong certified in adult physical therapy and general orthotics as I am certified in pediatric physical therapy.

Dottie turned around and said, "Mom and Dad, I present you Mister and Missus Abe and Beca Strong.

After a long visit, it was clear that the girls had worked with Beca in the Dallas Polio Center while Abe was finishing his six months in the orthotics department.

Abe was asked to explain what he did as an orthotist. "I start by measuring a patient for the type of brace he needs. You heard of the KAFO long leg brace with the flexing/locking knee; well we have the AFO, the FO, and the KO braces. Plus we have similar braces for the upper arms. We also have shoe lifts since children often get short legs from the affected polio side. Then we also prevent and treat polio scoliosis as well as idiopathic scoliosis. You probably wonder what brace is used for scoliosis, well it is called the CTLSO brace, or cervico-thoraco-lumbo-sacral-orthosis. There is a lot of info I can give you on scoliosis and would do so when the need arises."

Addie saw the interview coming to an end so she flashed a hip Xray at the Strongs. Abe looked at Beca and said, "Any doubt?" Beca looked at the Duo and Quad and said, "this is Legg-Perthes disease in a child. A terrible disease that lasts a long time." Abe added, "it is treated with a special long leg brace that anchors on the Iliac Crest and the pelvis. It is a two-rod long brace that attaches to the lower leg above the ankle and the mid-thigh. It usually is worn for two years or longer depending on the rate of healing." Brad then added, "well you had better see that patient for he is located on the medical ward."

Addie then added, "there is no doubt in our minds, if you wish to work with us, we would love to have you." "Yes thank you." Dottie then added, "we'll help you find an apartment and introduce you to the hospital staff." Brad then jokingly said, "how are your finances lately\?" Abe just about choked when he said, "Doc Huxley had to pay for our train tickets to get here, heh?" Addie then handed Abe a bank draft for $500. "This is your sign on bonus to help you move in and get started. Your salary will each be $2,000 a year or each $77 every two weeks. Officially you are starting today. Now where on earth are we to get all the braces you were talking about." "The answer is the March of Dimes. Presently they are furnishing the Dallas Medical Center with a complete line of polio braces including the Milwaukee Brace. I am certain if you wait, an organizational rep will soon call on you."

DAY NINE. The cafeteria was full of staff for their morning breakfast. Suddenly the telegraph messenger arrives and yells out, "emergency telegram for Addie Kelly." Brad hands the messenger two bits as Addie reads the gram. With total silence, Addie starts reading:

FROM DOCTOR HALLET--HEALTH COMMISSONER

A SPORADIC CASE OF POLIO IN DUMAS STOP

ZERO CASE A QUILT CLUB LEADER WITH INFLUENZA SYNDROME STOP

THREE DAYS LATER CLUB MEMBERS COME DOWN WITH POLIO WITH PARALYSIS STOP

TWO MILD CASES AND ONE MODERATE STOP

MODERATE CASE NEEDS EXTRA VENTILATION PROVIDED BY HUSBAND STOP

WILL ARRIVE IN ONE HOUR STOP

PLEASE ARRANGE FOR AMBULANCES AT RR YARD STOP

THE SCOURGE HAS BEGUN MAY GOD HELP US STOP

**

CHAPTER 5

The Breathing Center

There was a sickening calm in the cafeteria. It reflected a dread and fear of what was to soon pass. Dottie was first to speak as she said, "Susie, Louisa, and I will take control of those three patients but each of us need a trained nurse and a volunteer to appreciate learning on the job—as we follow the rule of see one, do one, and teach one." Addie then mentioned that she would work the on-call lists and provide a nurse and volunteer for each patient plus one orderly for all three patients—all to staff the evening and night shifts.

Brad was on the phone to dispatch two ambulances to the railroad terminal with instructions to use oxygen if they saw any cyanosis or a pulse greater than 120. His second call was to the power company. That is when he found out that the power company was planning a city blackout between 1PM and 4PM. When Brad explained about the patients in an iron lung, the power company's manager said that they had a portable generator that would run 24 hours on bottled propane. Being assigned to the courthouse and mayor's office, they would gladly move it to the hospital and set it outside the breathing center. The generator would be attached to the inside transfer switch so the breathing center staff could engage it themselves.

By the time the hour passed, Louisa's team included nurse Sandra and volunteer Marylyn, with Roland as the trio's orderly. Dottie and Susie would lead the other two teams made up of similar workers—again all trained but without actual experience. Everyone knew that Louisa and the girls would be responsible for providing a live experience for their assistants.

The emergency room came to a standstill as the classic sound of the ambulance bells pierced the air. When they arrived, the attendants rushed the more affected patient inside as the presumed husband had to provide a deep breath to the lady via mouth to mouth. That is when Louisa said, "my name is Louisa, this is Sandra, this is Marylyn, and this is Roland. We will now take over and will take care of you. To start with, breathe in this apparatus for a couple of breaths. Afterwards, Louisa said, "the air you moved was 125 ml instead of the expected maximum of 500 ml and the minimum to hold off the breathing machine would have been 325 ml. It is clear to me that you need to rest and breathe in our 'iron lung.' The husband added, "My name is Harold Holt. Doc Wilson in Dumas said she had 50% leg and arm paralysis and 75% of her chest wall muscles affected. He sent us here to use the breathing machine." After a short pause, Elaine Holt said, "Harold, I can no longer continue like this, I am ready for the 'iron lung' as it is called."

Roland did not lose any time as he whisked her in the wheelchair right next to the #1 labeled unit. Slowly and gently lifting her out of the wheelchair and placing her in the slide-out bed. In no time her neck was secured in the closing leather webbing and the machine started. After a half dozen cycled breaths, Elaine smiled and said, "my God, I can finally breathe, this is a miracle."

Harold was tearing and suddenly collapsed. It was Louisa who said, "Roland would you get Harold a cot, a blanket, and a pillow. This man is plumb worn out from giving his physical lifesaving breath to his wife. He now needs to get some rest." Elaine responded with a look of impending doom as Harold was on the floor. It was Marylyn who said, "not to worry, we'll take care of Harold. Your job is to get well for that is what Harold would want."

The gals had the other two victims in their own 'iron lung as the staff was learning how to care for them. The other husbands were sitting in a chair next to their wives' face. Two hours later Harold woke up in a panicking startled response. He rushed to Elaine's side and asked, "is she still with us?" Elaine opened her eyes and said, "why of course, I was just enjoying every breath. Looking at Sandra, she said, "I need to pee, so what do we do?" Marylyn said, "we'll take care of that. Harold was watching as Louisa and Marylyn opened the dome to put a bedpan inside the unit. Then four arms went thru the portholes with gloved hands as two lifted her body and two placed the bedpan under her bottom. At the end, Louisa did a quick wipe as the dome was again lifted to remove the bedpan. It was Louisa who said, "when we lift up the dome, if we are quick, you should not lose more than two breaths."

Harold saw all this and asked, "how do you know if your portholes are sealing enough and you are not losing air?" "Simple, look at the psi gage. If it reaches 40 psi on inhalation, the portholes are sealed." "Really, so if I watch the psi gauge, could I hold my wife's hand?" "Absolutely!"

Two hours later, Harold was still holding Elaine's hand. Addie arrived at noon sharp, gathered the three husbands and said, "with your wife in the iron lung, you are all welcome to stay with her 24/7. You also have a chair for daytime use and a cot/blanket/pillow for sleep. Plus you get three meals a day and coffee 24 hours a day. We provide apples for the morning and afternoon snacks. Now it is lunch time and your wives need to learn how to eat while still breathing. They need some privacy for their learning meal, so follow me to the cafeteria, heh?"

*

The afternoon was uneventful till 1PM when the power went off. To the husbands' surprise, the staff started running to disconnect the motor's transmission and then man the manual handle with hand and foot pedal to maintain ventilation. The staff kept the patients breathing for a solid hour till a man wearing electrician's clothing came inside and said, "you can all hear the new outside hum. That is a company generator to use till yours arrives. When the power goes out, in one minute you will hear the hum and all you have to do is pull this master transfer switch down and your breathing center will light up. When the power comes back up, lift the master transfer switch up and the generator will stop. Simple, foolproof, and safe, heh?"

Then came the 3PM change of shift. After extensive introductions, the new team was informed that the patients had experienced an oatmeal lunch, swallowing water, had experienced complete toileting, and were allowed to hold hands with their husbands. Supper would be hamburg, mashed potatoes, and hot coffee. Like water, all liquids were taken thru a straw but solid food was presented as a spoon or fork-full by the volunteers.

During the evening all three husbands were shown how to use the overhead rack to hold the daily newspaper. The ladies had it made, for the husbands had to stay nearby to turn the pages and again anchor the newspaper. The husbands stayed up to see the night shift. Again, after introductions, the new team was given the day's activities and what the patients still needed to learn. Afterwards, the husbands were glad to lay down and get some sleep. During the night, one of the ladies started her monthly cycle and was easily applied the necessary accessories.

By morning, the day shift came back. Louisa announced that the ladies would experience their first sponge bath at the hands of the workers without opening the dome. To ease their adventure, the husbands were sent to the cafeteria for breakfast, but were warned that tomorrow, they would be the ones to bathe their wives under specific instructions.

Meanwhile, Addie and Brad were busy. Without warning, the railroad delivered three more iron lungs and one more rocking bed. These had been fully assembled and tested by the distribution center. After setting them up in the breathing center, the Duo had a chat with each patient and their husbands. Since each patient did not have any bulbar manifestations, a full resuscitation status was established for all three patients.

That same day, three 8th graders who had attended a girl's birthday party, came down with polio. Dottie and Susie saw all three and with a tidal volume above the 65% minimal tidal volume of 163 ml; all three were admitted for observation since their extremities were minimally affected. It was midnight when the girl started crying as she claimed that she could barely move her legs and breathing had become very tiresome. Her tidal volume was again tested and was less than 100 ml. Without hesitation, she was moved into an iron lung and her parents were notified.

It was after the morning shift change that the boys both failed the tidal volume test and were transferred to their own machine. Throughout the day a new revelation was discovered. 8th grade boys ages +- 13-14 were extremely responsive to hands over their bodies. It became clear that the boys were coming to full salute and that the cuter the nurse, the worse was the response. Roland and his team of orderlies and male volunteers had a tall order to fill. It was quickly realized that full grown men caused less of a response than female attendants.

With six iron lungs occupied, three in reserve, and none on back order, Brad made the decision to authorize the three woodshop carpenters to build more wooden iron lungs. Since the carpenters had been busy cutting up plywood into the necessary pieces, plus having a good supply of leather, glass, and metal parts, they were able to put out a completed 'wooden iron lung' in an eight-hour period. Brad ordered three and waited out the days.

*

Fortunately for the next week no new cases appeared. The three spare iron lungs were set up on the female side of the room as the three wooden units were set up on the male side of the room. Harold and the two other husbands were walking around the wooden units. Addie saw them and decided to start the motor once the electrical plug was set in the outlet. All eyes turned toward the wooden coffins and everyone realized that although they did look like coffins, they would certainly keep the polio patients alive. The thing that gave these wooden units any credence was the fact that the plywood was stained a walnut color and the wood and stain smell was sealed with the new polyurethane coating that sealed off all odors.

For two weeks, the patients adapted to vegetative living except for one thing—muscle cramps and muscle pain. The pain was well controlled with therapeutic doses of aspirin as many home recipes for managing cramps were used. Two level teaspoons of the new condiment, yellow mustard, were the most effective because it contained acetic acid which was used to make acetylcholine: a precursor to muscle function. Bananas were full of magnesium, calcium, and potassium, but were hard to get in northern Texas. As a substitute for bananas, supplements of the three minerals, were given to polio victims to minimize muscle cramps. Elaine was suffering the most with thigh cramps. The Tenney moist packs were continually applied and massages were done each hour. Beca got close to that 8th grade gal and provided her mental and physical relief. The ladies got plenty of help from Abe and Roy (the regular hospital therapist), but Elaine had to periodically get an intramuscular injection of an anesthetic and muscle relaxant called 'intocostrine' (made from curare) every three or four days plus plenty of massage and moist heat packs.

Elaine's two lady friends were first to start weaning out of the iron lungs. As Elaine was just starting the weaning process, her two friends were already using the rocking beds with increasing times out of the iron lungs each day. It was clear to Dottie and Susie that these two ladies, who had only mild paralysis of the legs, would make it home without assistive devices. Elaine's slow progress and persisting weakness would require an orthotic for her to be ambulatory and independent—as long walking distances would need to be made by wheelchair.

*

As the facts were clear, the polio team was looking into procuring the assistive devices that Elaine would need. It was the same time when JD showed up with a gentleman wearing a striking purple shirt, white pants and a shirt logo that read 'March of Dimes.' Abe was quickly pulled out of the treatment center to be present at the meeting with the first orthotic rep to show up on the scene. The organization's man started to speak. "Hello Doctor and Missus Kelly, I am honored to finally meet you. My name is Yvon Hasselback and I represent your district as well as the Dallas district. As you know, we are a donation-based organization that was started to assist polio victims. In short, we will provide you with all the orthotics you will need to keep the polio victims as ambulatory as possible even down to the use of a free wheelchair. The only requirement is that you provide us with a room to store the devices and an orthotist to properly measure, care, educate patients, and repair the devices when they break or wear out." After more discussions, the Duo showed Yvon the storage room next to the rehab center and introduced him to Abe Strong.

Within four hours, three workers emptied three wagons of braces for legs, arms, and scoliosis as well as provide several wheelchairs for children and adults. As the March of Dimes team was leaving, Yvon handed Addie a list of prices that the March of Dimes was paying manufacturers for every brace and wheelchair delivered today. Yvon added, "In case some of your patients needing a device might consider making a donation—as any amount is always greatly appreciated, heh?" Addie never missed a step as she handed Yvon a bank draft in the amount of $500.

It was a week later when Abe put on a lecture on polio orthotics. To compensate for differing time shifts he repeated it that same evening.

"Thank you for coming. To begin, there is no doubt that the most commonly needed brace is the long leg device that allows ambulation and standing erect. Of course I am referring to the KAFO or the knee-ankle-foot-orthosis. This device goes from the mid-thigh to the foot. It provides support, joint flexibility, and minimizes pain. It is an innovative device that, with a snap of the foot's heel, allows flexion of the knee during ambulation. The knee hinge prevents the leg from buckling forward or backward at any time during walking or standing. It anchors in mid-thigh with a leather strap and in the calf with a similar strap. This device is being modified regularly and may not look like the same device from year to year."

"The other popular brace is the AFO to manage a foot drop which is common with mild cases of leg paralysis. The one we use fits inside the shoe and is not visible with pant legs. I may add we have a similar long arm brace that has elbow flexion controlled at the wrist and attaches in mid-upper arm and mid-forearm. Plus every brace comes in sizes for children and adults."

"While I am still on leg braces it is important to realize that most braces do not relieve pressure on the bones. Pressure on the growth plates is needed for extremities to grow in length. If the pressure is removed you end up with a short leg which causes a limp, a functional scoliosis, and bilateral hip pain. The cure are shoe lifts which start with insoles then change to exterior soles and heels for major short legs—a bit cumbersome and ugly but they work. A properly fitting orthotic brace provides support and functionality without stunting growth. Keep in mind that bone growth continues till the end of puberty which in girls is 13-15 and boys 15-17."

"Now polio scoliosis is caused by an uneven involvement and paralysis of the paraspinal muscles along the spine. For practical purposes it also includes idiopathic scoliosis in children but excludes the functional scoliosis caused by uneven legs. Most of the cases of polio scoliosis causes an outward curve above the T-7 level and is corrected by the CTLSO brace (cervico-thoraco-lumbo-sacral orthosis). For curves below T-7 to the sacrum there is another brace that starts at the low thorax area and ends at the sacrum (TLSO). Both braces have the same steel framework of double rods front and back, but the straps that apply pressure to a curve are located at different locations on the body."

"You all know that some things are not always simple and clearcut. Wearing a scoliosis brace causes abnormal dental changes—loss of facial height from a protrusion of anterior teeth and a reversal of posterior teeth. After wearing such a brace for a long period, orthodontic work will be needed to regain natural facial features."

"A scoliosis brace is needed if the curvature is 20-50 degrees. If it is greater than 50 degrees, the braces are of no help—especially if after puberty. A scoliosis brace is worn 23 hours a day and that 24th hour is to do the prescribed exercises. The common age for idiopathic scoliosis to appear is 10-18. On the average, teenagers will need to wear the brace for two years unless puberty occurs early. Juveniles will need to wear it longer because the growth plates are very active before puberty even starts."

"And so in closing, the good news is that the March of Dimes will provide these braces and wheelchairs free of charge. I will measure the patients who need one and if it is not in our inventory, the foundation will have one here overnight. Remember one thing, this foundation exists based on donations as the classic donation card includes slots for twenty 'dimes' or less. Even in the depression everyone can afford a dime for a good cause during the polio epidemic—that is why the card was so designed, heh? Plus for the well to do, a flap could be lifted to allow paper currency. As you leave please take a card and make a donation. I personally know that the Kellys have made a sizeable donation. Thank you for coming and that does it for today's lecture."

*

It was Marylyn who had documented Elaine's weaning schedule.

The first day she was out of the iron lung for one minute when she went into respiratory arrest. The next day was five minutes to abrupt respiratory arrest. The third day was ten minutes to respiratory fatigue, and the fourth day was 15 minutes to respiratory fatigue which was tolerated for another 15 minutes. Even if she tried to wean more quickly the progress did not change that same day. It took two weeks for Elaine to stay out of her iron lung for an hour and tough-out another hour of fatigue. That is when she graduated to the rocking bed. The same occurred with the rocking bed. It too required a weaning schedule made to fit the patient as it was so coming out of the iron lung. Since every patient was different, no set weaning schedule could be established for weaning from the iron lung or rocking bed. Plus, there was a test period when the patient had to stay in room air all day and even walk about the hospital several times a day before a patient could be discharged to home and the outpatient rehab center.

Elaine had been a resident for six weeks as her two friends and the teenagers were soon to be on their way home when the unexpected happened. Six card players from the Rusty Bucket Saloon appeared with 2nd degree moderate paralysis. Quick questioning revealed that all five players were with a sick saloon dealer who claimed to have a cold. Three days later the five players and the card dealer were in the emergency room. Also present was the saloon's owner, the one and only Aloysius Talbot—the shoe factory owner and surprise silent owner of the Rusty Bucket Saloon. All Addie could say was, "well this could be a long …!"

Seeing all six using up the three iron lungs and the three wooden iron lungs left nothing in reserve. Brad contacted the distribution center and found out that no iron lungs were available. He then went to see Mike at the woodshop. Mike was watching his six unemployed carpenters learning the trade of fabricating wooden iron lungs. Mike eventually explained, "I have signed a contract to provide wooden iron lungs to sell to the Houston distribution center for $100. Cost of materials is +- $20 and the cost of labor is +- $30. Shipping to Houston is $5 and I make a profit of $45 per unit. With nine men working, we should be able to produce three units a day as long as the plywood and accessories are available." Brad simply looked at Mike and said, "I'll take the first six units coming off your assembly line and here is the $600 to cover them."

Within a week, six wooden units were delivered to the Polio Center. They were added in line so that the breathing center was full of the 18 iron lungs of which half were the wooden kind. If the need ever increased to six more, the breathing center could hold a total of 24 iron/wooden lungs.

A few days later, six more victims appeared in the ER. A post service church social resulted in this crop of victims. Of which two were clearly victims of the 3rd degree. One could not swallow and one had droopy eyelids. Brad recollected that all 18 units were in use although the original three teenagers were ready for discharge and Elaine's friends were to follow. The surprise was that an astute nurse had detected a skipping pulse in one of Elaine's friends.

Doctor Greene was quick to arrive with the portable EKG machine. The tracing revealed a long QT interval, a wide QRS, elevated ST-T wave segment, and several PVCs—all acute changes that were not present on her admission EKG. A chest Xray revealed cardiomegaly (an enlarged heart) all diagnostic of a late myocarditis. The patient was immediately started on aspirin and procain as were all heart attack victims. Since the lady was a full resuscitation, the pulse alarm was placed on her arm during sleep times—which would beep loudly if her heartbeat stopped.

Over the next week the teenagers and one of Elaine's friends went home without assistive devices. Over another month, Elaine and her myocarditis friend finally made it home. Her friend's heart had decreased in size and the EKG changes were disappearing. She went home on long term aspirin and at least a month's worth of procain. The girls would follow the myocarditis lady in their outpatient offices. Elaine went home with two KAFO orthotics and was well trained in their proper use. For long walking events, she had her reliable wheelchair at her side.

No one knew that Harold had had a private meeting with Angus, the hospital accountant. Harold first asked, "what is the daily cost for a patient in the breathing center?" "$8 a day!" Well add it up, my wife was 3 ½ months here, she got two leg braces and a wheelchair. Her two friends were here 2 and 2 ½ months. In my book that comes to +-236 total days. At $8 a day that comes to $1888. I presume this bank draft will take care of the extra expenses of housing and feeding three men for the duration. Harold handed Angus the bank draft and walked out before Angus could protest.

Two days later, Addie came up to Harold and handed him a bank draft for $3112. "Paying the bill in full for three ladies was way more than we expected. This is your money!" "No it is a tip to the Kelly Hospital for giving me my wife back. Do you realize that Elaine spent 3 ½ months here and not one day did your nurses or volunteers ignore her. I am a wealthy man with a lot of clout in the political arena, so keep the extra three grand, for you will certainly need to fund the expansion you will soon experience." Addie was so shocked that she froze in place as Harold waved goodbye. Little did she know that Harold had made Mike Waters an offer he could not refuse as he also bought a wagon to bring Elaine home with her own wooden iron lung.

*

With the teenagers all home as well as the three first ladies, that left the six gamblers in the iron lungs as some were fortunate to start weaning two weeks into their treatment. Mike arrived one morning and delivered the six prepaid wooden units. The twelve existing units were moved to allow six more in the breathing center. Before Mike left, Brad gave him another $600 for six more units to be in reserve storage over the 18 units in place.

Time seemed to move along slowly as the Duo got yancy over the Polio Center investment. Dottie and

Susie both encouraged Addie that time would confirm the need for Kelly Hospital's preemptive investment. So, now four weeks since the gamblers entered the center, Aloysius Talbot appeared at Addie's office. Without even saying hello he said, "well my employee and five gamblers have been here a month. Time to settle their accounts. So give me a final bill for all six!" Addie was not about to be rolled over so she said, "each man stayed 30 days at $8 a day comes to $240 per man or for six comes to $1440." "Yes mathematically it comes to $1440 but don't you give a discount for local merchants?" "Yes, but that is our prerogative to help our people. But you Sir are a member of a hostile council. So unless you are not satisfied with the care we gave your employee and customers, you may choose to ignore your financial responsibilities but your name will be placed on the local blacklist of non-paying parasites." Needless to say, Talbot produced a $1440 bank draft and walked out without uttering another word.

It was a slow week with an empty breathing center. Other than the teenagers and Elaine doing their therapy in the rehab center, the gals were following Elaine's friend with the myocarditis. It was on one of those visits that the Duo was informed of a perfect storm about to happen. Apparently boredom was hitting the ranches in the panhandle as many took the train to Pueblo for a weekend of entertainment. Gathering in restaurants, saloons, theatre, and dance halls was a perfect set up for spreading the polio virus.

It was a week later that the first call came in the ER. Mister True of the railroad told Doctor Titus that four family members were on the train heading to Amarillo—a husband and wife and two grandparents. All four had polio and were escorted by cowboys as human crutches to help them walk— as an older man was in a wheelchair. Doctor Titus released two ambulances to the railroad terminal. Mister True then notified the ER staff that all trains heading to Amarillo would have a wheelchair for each passenger car till the end of the polio epidemic.

Addie was next to be notified. As the administrator with all the phone numbers, she called in Dottie, Susie, Louisa, and three other nurses as well as four volunteers—two men and two ladies. The team opened the breathing center, checked the function of four iron lungs, and waited for the arrivals in the ER.

Two taxis arrived as the older gent was placed in a taxi transferring chair, and the three others were helped into the ER. Four wheelchairs were waiting as all four new patients were deposited in hospital wheelchairs. Every patient, as they sat down, was moaning in relief. The young man said, "we are the Maxwells, Sam, Ginny, Elfreda, and Homer. We were sent here by our country doctor for the breathing machines."

All four arrivals were given the spirometer to measure their tidal volume. All four were below the 65% TV and all qualified for the breathing machine. When Louisa asked, "is your breathing work getting unbearable. All heads nodded in the positive. Plus the older gent added, "before we left home, my doctor reminded me that I have end stage silicosis from mining dust and I am requesting that if my heart stops, please let me go."

The four were placed in the iron lungs and allowed to breathe for an hour. Then the admitting ritual started. Doctor Greene drew blood, did an EKG, and a Chest Xray. The patients were taught when to speak and when to swallow. They then had their first oatmeal feast, had a full sponge bath, changed into button-up scrubs, helped with urination, and told how toileting would be done. Last of all they were started on Aspirin to control pain, had moist hot packs applied, and given two level teaspoons of yellow mustard for muscle cramps. Next, they were introduced to the hospital's physical therapy group. Last of all a clarified resuscitation status was established for the other three members. Once that was all accomplished, the medical staff was stunned to see a cowboy enter the breathing center as he said, "the cowboys are soon to take the last train back home, but what are we to do with the 10- and 13-year-old boy and girl with us in the rehab center waiting room?" You could have dropped and heard a feather as everyone had not had the sense to ask if they had any kids. Beca stepped forward and said, "not to worry, I will take care of that."

After the trauma of seeing mom, dad, and both gramps in those machines, Todd and Cindy adjusted quickly. They started eating in the cafeteria, shared a double observation room, eventually graduated to a cot beside their parents, and started contributing to their family's care.

*

The days went by and the explosion started. At first it seemed to be single sporadic cases, then it was transmitting it to loved ones, and finally to more groups gathering in Pueblo for a holiday weekend. Plus, a diner in town got several patrons sick from a cook that had the flu. The bottom line, all 18 iron and wooden lungs were occupied as Mike delivered another six which were put in storage—using the first observation room to keep the units close by."

It was two weeks with 100% occupancy and just another regular day as Doctors Reinhart and Tisdale were doing their daily checks for lung congestion and atelectasis, as well for decubitus ulcer and signs of a urinary tract infection. Dottie and Susie were doing inspiratory checks to see if anyone was ready for weaning.

Out of a peaceful quietude came a piercing sound from hell. The catastrophe siren had been rung by Doctor Titus. Suddenly, Nancy Grover appeared, at the entrance of all four active wards, and yelled out, **"CODE D, THIS IS NOT A DRILL. ALL AVAILABLE STAFF AND ALL DOCTORS TO THE ER ....NOW!"**

Addie looked at Louisa as she said, "that does not include you, your nurses, and your volunteers. Maintain care as if nothing has happened. Your responsibilities are here in this room." Louisa added, "but I have two volunteers who are O negative!" "Oh, well send them to the ER but they will be back." Addie turned around and headed to the ER to find out what the catastrophe was and how the triage was being assigned.

**

CHAPTER 6

CODE D

Addie arrived in the ER as Doctor Titus announced to everyone, "the sheriff just called me to say that the town circus/fair had a shooting. Apparently the attendant at a shooting gallery got in an argument with a shooting customer. Allegedly the shooter was not aiming for the knock down targets but was shooting at the wooden shelves as he and his buddy were turning the shelves to splinters. The attendant got perturbed and took a rifle and butt-plated the leader in the forehead as his buddy pulled out a handgun. Well the attendant shot the buddy between the eyes, went amuck, lifted the rifle, and proceeded to randomly shoot at the crowd walking by. By the time the attendant was emptying the second rifle, someone drew their peacemaker and shot the attendant in the heart. Despite the shooter's end, four bystanders were dead, and 10 were critically wounded as another dozen or more had varying degrees of gunshot wounds—some with life threatening blood loss."

Finishing his info, he did not take questions as he ordered four general surgeons and one orthopedic surgeon to the OR with OR nurses, nurse anesthetists, the OR supervisor nurse, and a full team of recovery nurses. The medical doctors were all assigned to start IV's, draw blood, and apply oxygen to the patients heading to the OR. Afterwards the medical doctors would be assigned to the suturing staff which included the two obstetricians. Nurses were assigned to each doctor as assistants while the ER nurses were the gophers to get this and that. Once everyone was assigned, they all waited in anticipation.

During these preparations, Doctor Greene was already collecting O negative blood from the two polio center volunteers. As the main welcoming desk was still calling medical staff at home, Addie was busy calling other O negative blood donors. By the time preparations were finished, the medical doctors had a total of 12 IVs ready for cannulation with normal saline and portable oxygen tanks were at the ready.

The first two ambulances had four chest gunshot wounds. Doctor Titus labeled the first stable and to follow. The second was in respiratory distress, his trachea deviated to the left, his right chest was expanded inappropriately and had no auscultated breath sounds. Doctor Titus took a large bore needle and inserted it in the 4th-5th intervertebral space. The loud gush of air gave the distressed patient some quick relief. Doctor Titus then ordered this patient with a tension pneumothorax as the first case for the waiting surgeons.

The next two chest gunshot victims were evaluated and the one with severe shock was on oxygen and had two IVs started—one for saline and one for the O negative blood transfusion. The shock victim was next to the operating room. The other two chest gunshot victims were moved to the recovery room for careful monitoring while waiting for time in the OR.

The next ambulance had three chest gun shots and one abdominal gunshot. The one with the abdominal wound had no blood pressure and was in extremist shock. With the bullet hole in the upper left abdominal quadrant, it was clear that the spleen had been hit. Doctor Norwood ordered quick divinyl ether anesthesia as he grabbed a scalpel and performed an opening laparotomy as he placed a clamp on the splenic artery. With oxygen, blood, and saline running, the patient was whisked to the OR with a Kelly clamp sticking out of his belly. On Arrival, Brad broke scrub and with anesthesia, took over the emergency splenectomy but saved the running of the intestines for later.

After stabilizing the other three chest gunshot wounds, all three were moved to the recovery room with a tag on them to denote their pending status. Despite the tag, if the recovery room nurses detected a more unstable patient, that one took precedence. That left two more with tourniquets on legs because of arterial bleeds. Those became priority since a limb could be lost if the tourniquet was not periodically released. The last two with serious gunshots were gut-shot victims in moderate pain. Both of those were started on IVs, given morphine for the pain, and sent to the recovery room to wait their turn. The last two cases were gun- shots to the shoulder and another to the elbow. Both of those were cleansed, IVs started and sent to the recovery room. The major injury was in a 12-year-old girl with a shattered shoulder.

That left a dozen or more minor gunshot victims. Some had thru and thru gunshots and some still had a bullet in the wound. The two obstetricians were assigned the ones who needed probing to remove the bullet. The four medical doctors were assigned the ones that needed cleansing with carbolic acid and noncomplicated suturing.

Meanwhile, the four general surgeons were practicing WW1 lifesaving surgery. No one knew that several observers were documenting the events in the ER and the drama in the ORs. Included in the ER were Mister True of the railroad, Mister Gregory, and Mayor Monroe. Hidden from view was Aloysius Talbot sneaking a peek from the hospital side of the

ER entrance. Later no one realized that he managed to steal away to the OR suite and witnessed the drama that unfolded to save lives.

*

After the five surgeons scrubbed, they added the standard surgical gowns and gloves and waited for the first patient. Doctor Tom Hall was teamed with his son Eric and Jimmy was teamed with his dad. It was Tom, with WW1 experience in a first line hospital on the front, who laid down today's rules of surgical engagement. "Let me be very clear. We need to save lives and not take precious time to preserve mutilated tissues. So we need to move from one patient to another without doddering. That means we enter the chest as close as possible to the entrance bullet hole, make a long 10-inch intercostal incision, apply the self-retaining rib retractors, cauterize bleeders, identify the bleeding lobe of lung, clamp off the main bronchiole tube and blood vessels, remove the lobe with blunt dissection, extract the bullet if it did not go thru the back side, leave a chest tube, and get out.

Pull the retractor, let the patient be moved sideways, and let Doctor Scanlon suture the intercostal muscles, and install the suction and air trapping bottles. While you drape the next patient and repeat the procedure. In other words, QI--QO (quick in and quick out)." Brad then added, "the head surgeons are Jimmy and Eric, we dads will be your assistants."

When the first patient arrived, he was placed under anesthesia with the new form fitted hard rubber face mask attached to a rubber air bag which allowed free flow of the anesthetic gas. The rubber bag also allowed a hand squeezed high pressure ventilation as requested by the surgeons to test a tied off bronchial tube—as Dottie was considering using this new ventilating bag for transferring polio victims.

The anesthetists were using the two new non-flammable anesthetic gases, trichlorethylene/nitrous oxide combination with oxygen. They provided a quick induction without depressing respiration, an easy recovery from anesthesia, and a safe usage of the new electro cautery for quick hemostasis instead of the slow tying off of each bleeder.

That first patient still had a large air venting bore needle in a lower intercostal and as soon as the anesthetist gave the go-ahead signal, Jimmy made a single pass in the intercostals next to the bullet hole. Brad was pushing hard to get the intercostal muscles bleeders under control with the electric cautery as Jimmy applied the rib retractors and shoved both hands in the patient's chest. After asking for a large clamp, he did a quick blunt dissection and pulled out a macerated right upper lobe. Brad then located the bullet imbedded in a rib and after cauterizing and sterilizing the site, helped Jimmy use varying sizes of triple bonded nylon sutures from size #1 for the bronchiole tube down to the smaller 1 to 3-O nylon for arteries and veins. With hemostasis and without leaking air under a high-pressure manual ventilation, the retractor was pulled and Jimmy asked for the next case.

The head nurse said, "we have an abdominal wound with a bleeding spleen with shock, and a chest wound with heavy bleeding with shock. Jimmy said, "Dad, do the splenectomy and I'll start on the next thoracotomy—it won't be the first time I do one alone, heh?" So Brad did the splenectomy and left running the bowel till later. When Brad went back to Jimmy's thoracotomy, he was dissecting a right middle lobe out. After tying off the stump, Doctor Scanlon was doing Eric's two thoracotomy suturing and Jimmy's two chest cases as well. It was at that time that Talbot had been watching the drama in the OR as Jimmy and Eric asked for their third cases.

*

Throughout the entire afternoon and evening, Doctor Greene stayed in the OR or the recovery room keeping patients hemodynamically stable. By monitoring the blood pressure, pulse, and occasional blood hematocrit levels, he would vary the rate of the saline infusion versus supplementing them with O negative blood. With his lab assistant running the initial blood studies, he would add necessary deficient minerals in the IV infusion. The result was that the surgeons did not need to monitor the level of anesthesia or the need for certain IVs or blood as they could concentrate on what they were trained to do—life saving surgery.

As it happened from hour to hour, differing cases went thru the operating theatre. When the last cases arrived, Doctor Greene moved over to the recovery room where he found several of the medical doctors hovering over the fresh post-op patients. It was Dottie and Susie's decision to move the three most unstable patients to the Intensive Care Unit where Doctor Greene could do X Rays and run more blood tests.

The last case of the day was a gunshot to the head of a 40-year-old farmer and father of five. The wound entered on the right forehead and exited out of the rear occiput. The five surgeons were discussing the management when Jimmy said, "this man has been waiting seven hours with a bandage on his wound. He is still alert but the damaged brain will continue bleeding and will get infected. Eric and I have had some extensive experience removing a skull plate, cauterizing bleeders, and removing damaged tissues which would be the nidus of infection. We have nothing to lose and if we do nothing this will end up a fatal event. We are willing to try to save this man."

The procedure started with a bloody scalp incision that put the cautery to good use. With a scalp flap, the outer skull layer was exposed. With careful work a large skull plate was cut out and removed to a sterile saline dish for future use. Brad and Tom were stunned to see a live brain. There were bleeders that were controlled with the cautery and extensive debridement of unsalvageable tissues. With good hemostasis, the skull plate was trimmed and reapplied much looser than the original plate. This allowed for brain edema. The scalp flap covered the bone plate and skin edges were sutured together. Post operatively, a hypertonic saline solution was made by Doctor Greene. This hyperosmolar infusion created an osmotic gradient that drew cerebral edema fluid as it also decreased intracranial pressure—the two conditions that hampered recovery.

It was 9PM when the surgical team was closed down. With the bulk of the post-op patients stable in either the recovery room or the ICU, the team was allowed to get a delayed supper in the cafeteria. All the doctors were sitting together over fresh coffee as Brad said the first words. "Well this day will go down the books as the day that proved our lot as modern doctors. I saw some innovative medical medicine, fancy surgery, and some fine individual techniques. As far as I am concerned you have all 'made your bones' like credible modern doctors. I am proud of you as I am certain that the remainder of us 'old timer docs' feel the same way." Tom was first to say, " here, here!"

There was a lot of small talk as Tom finally said, "well Titus, did you know that the large bore needle that looked like a trocar could easily pass as a weapon—but as a painful jab as it was, you saved two young men's lives. Doctor Greene added his jab when he said, "and what about you Doc Norwood, I didn't know that obstetricians even knew where the spleen was say nothing of finding the splenic artery, heh?" More laughter and applause. After the laughter quieted down, Tom said, "all kidding aside that was some bold and beautiful neurosurgery we all saw."

The friendly jabs continued as most doctors were tapped. The jovial joking came to an abrupt stop when the meal was served.

*

The next morning at daybreak saw a team of phlebotomists and X Ray technicians at work. Blood was being drawn for typing, crossmatching, red and white blood counts, electrolytes, and kidney functions. X Rays were taken of the chest in all post thoracotomy patients as well as abdominal X Rays in all post laparotomy patients. This was the minimum testing till surgical rounds were done. Each patient's labs were placed in the chart and the X Rays displayed on the viewing box. Jimmy and Eric were leading the team that included Brad, Tom, Doc Greene, Doc Scanlon, Dottie, and Susie. The boys had an open discussion and outlined their plan for each patient's day. Then they asked the team for comments or alternative plans. That is when things got dicey.

When a team is made up of well-meaning experts, then everyone has their own way to 'skin the cat.'

Jimmy and Eric, having done their training with prima-donna instructors, had learned diplomacy— let the so-called experts speak and then take every idea into consideration. Pick and choose but always make changes to accommodate someone's therapeutic regimen which could benefit the patient and put aside the different ways to skin the cat—although you might use their regimen in the future. It was now 48 hours since the CODE D upheaval. The eight thoracotomy patients were all moved to the specialized surgery ward in the multi-patient ward where special observation and care was provided before private room care. The surgical team made up of Brad, Tom, Addie, and doctors Greene, Scanlon, Dottie, and Susie were following the surgeons of record—Jimmy and Eric. When they arrived at the third patient, Jimmy said, "let's stop a moment and go over the salient issues we like to cover on rounds—especially with this patient who is a candidate to have his chest tube removed at 48 hours." Eric started, "You all know that we start our rounds by addressing the patient, reviewing the morning chest X Ray, blood tests, the record's vital sign chart, and read the nurses notes. Then we apply the patient to the accepted criteria for early chest tube removal which are:

1. No air bubbles or fluid in the collection bottles for at least 12 hours.
2. Patient can maintain a full tidal volume for sex, age, and size and can take a deep breath with a doubled tidal volume.
3. The morning chest X Ray is clear of atelectasis (small peripheral lung tissue collapses), infiltrates of pneumonia, a pneumothorax (free air between the lung and chestwall), and free of effusions (tissue edema or blood) free floating between the lung and chest wall.
4. The patient passes the eight-hour test—the chest tube is clamped for eight hours and no changes occur in the patient's condition or in the repeat chest X Ray. During this time, the patient is allowed to sit in a chair and walk to the bathroom as he is carefully observed.

Addie was surprised and said, "why are we rushing, the standard time to pull the tube is 72 hours." Eric answered, "like a wound drain, if it is not draining in 48 hours, we pull it to prevent it becoming a foreign body that acts as a nidus for developing an infection. Same philosophy with chest tubes, when it no longer functions to remove air or fluid we pull it. In the long run, we might need to put it back in but the living statistics are in favor of early tube extraction." The team then added their thoughts as Jimmy and Eric filed the alternative regimens for future use.

At the end of the post thoracotomy rounds, the surgical team disbanded and Jimmy and Eric held their usual daily Q & A with the nursing staff. The questions were proof that nurses wanted more than just providing patient care, they wanted to know things and were not afraid to ask. That day, the two lead surgeons had to think before they spoke.

"What happens to the space where the lobes were removed?" "In time the space fills with lung tissue from the adjoining lobe. Just remember, the lung is like a sponge, it can expand as the intrathoracic pressure inflates the remaining lung tissue during breathing."

"Patients with upper lobectomies seem to recover quicker than those with central or lower lobectomies. Why is that?" "Because the diameter of the chest varies from the clavicle to the 10th rib. The upper chest has the least expansion where the ribs are the shortest, and so with least pain on breathing. You all know that pain is one of the major factors that delays healing—which is why we use so much frequent small doses of morphine."

"When you remove the chest tube, how long do you leave that large purse string nylon suture in place?" "If kept clean and sterilized daily with iodine, then we leave it in place for two weeks—depending on work restrictions. This is not the place to get a leak we assure you!"

"Since this patient's chest tube was clamped at 6AM and gets pulled today at 2PM, when can we transfer him to a private room?" "Tomorrow, after our rounds, and with our approval."

"All of these chest gunshots have a post-op temperature that hovers between 99 and a 100. When do we get alarmed and notify you?" "Assuming that you are not masking a fever with aspirin, then a temperature of 100.4 is pathological and we should be notified."

"Now we know why you do not prescribe aspirin in the first four days after surgery. You use frequent small doses of morphine to control the pain and not mask a pathological body temperature." "Correct, and that is a classic example how nurses today get informed compared to the old way of 'follow my orders blindly and don't ask why.'"

"What is the long-range prognosis for patients after a lobectomy?" "Recovery is complete and without disability or restrictions."

"Let's take a case where the bottles continue trapping air or fluids, what do you do?" Jimmy answered, "Eric and I wait a total of five days and then we reexplore the surgical site for an answer."

There was a long pause as the Q & A session was winding down. It was an older night nurse who finally spoke. "I have been around for a long time and I remember when the nurse's job was to sit with the family of a chest, abdomen, or head gunshot to wait for death while administrating laudanum orally or injecting morphine. I must say, it is a pleasure to still be working with young dynamic doctors that now save all these lives."

*

It was another week when the victims of the mass shooting were all discharged to home. Out of the blue, an incredible letter appeared in the local daily newspaper which read:

A LETTER OF UNREQUITED PRAISE

It is still fresh in your minds how this community suffered from a mass shooting. We are all appreciative of this unnamed cowboy who stepped up and put down this insane shooter. Yet do you know why, except for the four deaths at the scene, we did not lose anyone else after the victims arrived at our local hospital—with historically fatal gunshot wounds to the chest, abdomen, and head?"

Well, let us explain. Three of us were witnesses to the crisis occurring before our eyes. The ER was flooded with near death gunshots to the chest. Doctor Titus was a masterful triage officer who saved two such patients and ordered the most unstable victims to the OR where five surgeons were waiting. By the time the victims arrived in the OR they all had oxygen, IVs, and blood transfusions running thanks to Doctor Greene and every medical doctor on staff. It is also of note that a well-known obstetrician saved one man's life when he opened the abdomen and clamped off a bleeding splenic artery. That man was wheeled to the OR with a huge clamp sticking out of his belly. Looking back we did not expect this man to survive but he did and is well today. Once the critical patients were stabilized, they were all moved to the recovery room where they were monitored and the most critical patients went to the operating room as per highest immediate need.

At the same time, Aloysius Talbot had sneaked into the operating room theater and managed to get a look inside the OR. He witnessed surgeons entering an anesthetized patient's chest and deftly removing a mutilated lung lobe as the surgeons moved over to another victim on the edge of death. Doctor Scanlon was the cleanup surgeon to suture the chest cavity closed and insert a chest tube for post-op care.

After the chest gunshot lobectomies were done, the surgeons ran intestines looking for bullet holes to oversew as one older surgeon did some arterial repairs to avoid leg amputations. Doctor Scanlon then did a shoulder repair to save a 12-year-old girl's shoulder joint. The last operation of the day was a shocking brain exposure to stop bleeding and do some debridement before replacing a skull bony plate to close the head. Did anyone ever realize how sophisticated our new young surgeons had become?

While the drama continued in the OR and recovery room, there were at least fifteen or more victims with non-life-threatening gunshot wounds in the ER. It was a sight to see four medical doctors, two obstetricians and an ER doc debride, probe for detritus, irrigate, sterilize, and suture those fifteen patients of which four were admitted for observation.

Looking back, every hospital worker had been called in to participate in the victims' care. It was something to see 150 workers all working together to manage this disaster. That is the story and how our medical people saved everyone.

In closing, has anyone thought how we could thank our health care workers. To us it is very simple. Amidst this Great Depression, we must KEEP THIS HOSPITAL OPEN. As for the city council, one philanthropist, and two major employers, we will provide this hospital a subsidy that will cover any unpaid hospital or physician bills from this mass shooting disaster or from the polio center.

In addition, this letter is being sent to our Governor Rust in Austin. With the letter is an application requesting that he declare Kelly Hospital a Regional Medical Center. If we qualify, there will be a state subsidy that is shared with all the Texas Medical Centers.

Let's not forget that during this disaster, our polio breathing center continued operations. We now have 24 iron/wooden lungs that serve the panhandle's 26 counties and beyond as we are at 100% occupancy. At this same time the Walters carpenters are demolishing four more observation rooms and extending the breathing center to hold another dozen wooden iron lungs. And who is paying for all this care? PS. Of note is that every medical and surgical doctor on staff at the Kelly Hospital was trained at the Dallas Regional Medical Center.

Respectfully: Mayor Ulysses Monroe, Mister Gregory, Benjamin True railroad general manager, and Aloysius Talbot c/o Talbot Shoe Factory and Rusty Bucket Saloon.

*

Weeks went by and things settled down. The hospital census was still down as the Polio Center was at full capacity. It seemed as if the new arrivals had more brainstem involvement without the ability to swallow even water. Faced with the need for continuous IV therapy to maintain hydration, it was clear that would not provide enough nutrition to promote healing. So Jimmy and Eric started implanting feeding tubes thru the abdominal wall to the stomach. Doc Green made a liquid concoction to provide a high caloric content to include sugar, electrolytes, fiber, protein, water, and fat. That way each polio patient would get at least 2,400 nutritious calories per day. Following the schedule of small feedings every two hours, from morning to bedtime, were usually well tolerated. Each feeding was 200 ml and was fully gravity fed as long as there was no residual from the last feeding—12 feedings equaled 2,400 calories.

Months went by as the breathing census held at full occupancy of 24 patients in iron or wooden lungs and in differing stages of weaning. The Duo was beginning to think that referrals would not occur till the Depression started to resolve. It was at that time that an emergency telegram arrived for Addie. The messenger could not avoid saying, "this is the first time I ever delivered a gram from the Texas Governor's office." Addie read the message as the messenger asked, "any answer?" "Yes, send a note that we will be ready on said date."

Addie walked over to the doctors' offices and handed Brad the message with a shaking hand. Brad read it out loud.

FROM THE OFFICE OF THE TEXAS GOVERNOR STOP

TO ADELLE KELLY--KELLY HOSPITAL CEO STOP

GOVERNOR NORMAN RUST WILL VISIT YOUR HOSPITAL   STOP

SAVE THE DATE OF APRIL 1. 1935 FROM 1PM TO 9PM   STOP

WILL NEED AN ELEVATED STAGE AND SEATING FOR 300   STOP

PLEASE PROVVIDE SUPPER FOR 10 DIGNATARIES AND SPOUSES AND 10 SPECIAL GUESTS WITH SPOUSES   STOP

SAVE 20 FRONT ROW SEATS FOR YOUR MEDICAL STAFF AND SPOUSES   STOP

SAVE 20 SECOND ROW SEATS FOR SPECIAL GUESTS/SPOUSES   WOULD APPRECIATE GUIDED TOURS ON AFTERNOON OF DATE FOR THE DIGNATARIES AND THE SPECIAL GUESTS BEFORE THE EVENING SUPPER AND CEREMONIES   STOP

OPEN THE EVENING CEREMONIES TO THE ENTIRE MEDICAL STAFF   STOP

Brad looked at Addie and simply said, "looks like we have a week to get ready for who knows what. Guess we'd better start with Mike Walters to build us an elevated stage and install a speaker system which you have wanted for some time, heh?" Addie added, "and what are you going to do?" "Keep my nose to the grindstone and pretend this hoopla is not happening. You know I hate this more than discussing money!" "Well this is going to cost you a bucket of special personal favors, heh?" "Oh heck, as I recall this is only the fourth bucket and I managed to empty the first three with much pleasure for all, heh?" "For sure!"

*

As usual, things were ready when April 1st arrived. At 1PM two State Marshals entered and did a walk around to assure security. With their approval the entrance doors to the receiving rotunda were open. Addie and Brad received everyone as they introduced themselves and a badge was formed with everyone's name. After the dignitaries and special guests were all signed in, a free for all ensued as the remainder of the medical staff joined in. Addie and Brad encircled Doctor Carl Huxley and a nostalgic discussion followed. The real surprise was the invited guests. These represented 10 of the 20 'Country Docs' distributed over the panhandle's 26 counties—for 10 had to remain to cover those on holiday.

The socializing was summarized by an elderly doctor from Dumas as he said, "I sent you a minor stroke patient and you saved his life with a carotid endarterectomy. Plus I sent Doctor Hall a patient with blood in the urine and he removed a bladder cancer without invasive surgery. Now I am here to see two of my polio patients that I sent to your breathing center, to see your hospital, and participate in supper and the festivities."

The entire medical staff of doctors were the official guides as each one was used to answer questions that applied to the differing departments. Stepping into the breathing center was the epitome of 'shock and awe'. Both Dottie and Susie took turns explaining the iron and wooden lungs, the patients care, daily routines, the weaning process, and displaying the many orthotics already fitted for many of the patients. Once the presentation was done, the visiting doctors walked up to their specific patients and an amazing visit occurred. Everyone heard things like, "hi Doc what are you doing here?" "Why I came to see you and see how they are treating you?" "Why they are taking care of all my needs and I am getting better. Thank you for sending me to these angels for breathing is truly the gift of God."

The stay in the breathing center turned out to be a two-hour party as finally Addie announced that supper was served in the cafeteria. As they were all seated Mister Gregory said grace, the Duo wondered what was in store for this hospital once the festivities started and everyone found out what the Texas Governor was doing in a small city and an even smaller hospital.

**

CHAPTER 7

The Kelly Medical Center

During supper, one of the governor's staff was busy applying names to chairs—the first row for the medical staff and the second row for the visiting doctors—and for all their spouses. Once dessert was served that same staff member advised the local medical staff to take the time to dress up in their best attire.

Brad was in a fancy three-piece suit as Addie was in a floor length flared gown with plenty of cleavage and bare shoulders. Before they left Brad said, "my gosh, don't you look lovely and with plenty of decadence for all to enjoy. It is amazing how you look today compared to the day I pulled you out of that muddy river with mud all over your private parts, heh?" "Now dear, get your mind out of the gutter, we are going to some gala festivities—and we need to find out who is responsible for it, heh?"

As they arrived, the governor's staff were seating people. The medical staff were seated in the front row as the visiting doctors were seated in the second row. Nurses and accessory staff were seated as first come first seated behind the guests of honor. The last people seated were the dignitaries seated on the elevated stage to include: Governor Rust, Mayor Monroe, Mister Gregory, Benjamin True, Aloysius Talbot, Yvon Hasslebach of the March of Dimes, Sterling Cassidy of Texas Mutual Insurance, Doctor Carl Huxley of the Dallas Medical Center, and Doctor George Hallett, the panhandle's 26 county health commissioner.

With everyone seated a stillness fell amongst the hundreds of medical professionals in attendance. Everyone knew that whoever got up to start the proceedings would be the culprit who made it all happen. With no one getting up, the governor stood and said, "Doctor Hallett this is your creation, so please start the proceedings. Doctor Hallett stood and walked to the podium. "Ladies and gentlemen and doctors and nurses, I have been trying to have this evening for months and the letter that came out about the mass shooting gave me the chance to call this gathering."

"We put doctors on a pedestal, we respect them and follow their directives and in return we expect them to perform on our behalf. But how often do we publicly thank them? Not often enough. Well tonight is the exception. From an ad hoc committee of your peers we have established the next five awards."

"First for going back in training and starting three new surgical specialties we have Doc Scanlon in Orthopedic Surgery, Doc Kelly Sr. in vascular surgery, and Doc Hall Sr. in Urology." Under loud applause, the three doctors graciously accepted their awards.

"Our second award goes to a doctor that is never appreciated. Amongst you is a man who wore many hats over the past 30 years. He started as a phlebotomist, a laboratory technician, moved on to starting IVs and transfusing blood, to X Ray technician, EKG technician, master interpreter of

EKGs and X Rays and now one who has concocted a tube feeding and a hyperosmolar solution to control brain edema. All thru the years the only pathologist among your midst. Of course I am referring to the one and only Doctor Daniel Greene." This time the room gave him a standing ovation with loud applause till he accepted his award.

"Our third award goes to two young surgeons just out of training. With incredible speed and surgical finesse, they managed to save the lives of 8 chest gunshot victims. Not only a year ago, these would all have been fatal wounds. After that ordeal, they saved three victims of gunshot wounds to the intestines—another fatal wound in recent years. After ten grueling hours, they operated on a man who was shot in the head. Just below the stage is a family standing with five kids and a proud mom and dad. That dad is the head gunshot victims who is well today and back at work to support his family. So you all know who I am talking about—the Doctors James Kelly and Eric Hall. Be proud and come gather your awards." Another standing ovation with applause beyond belief.

"The fourth award goes to two modern medical doctors who volunteered for months in the Dallas Polio Center to learn the care of paralyzed victims treated in the iron lungs. Together with their mom, they started the breathing center with six iron lungs. Today it is running at 100% occupancy with 24 active polio victims under their care. Of course I am referring to the two ladies, Doctor S. Norwood-Kelly, and Doctor D. Kelly-Hall. Please step up for your awards." This time there were whistles, applause, and guffaws in appreciation.

"To not bore you I have only one more award. Although I could easily have added several more to honor the dedicated excellent work of Doctors Titus, Reinhart, Tisdale, and Weiss in OB/Gynecology."

"No I have not forgotten anyone, during the CODE D a doctor went beyond the call of duty. Whatever possessed an obstetrician to take a blade, open a dying man's abdomen, and find a splenic artery. He applied a large Kelly clamp and stopped the bleeding. The entire ER staff and receiving OR staff are still talking about a near comatose young male with a large Kelly clamp sticking out of the wound. Well that young man is alive because of the one and only our Doc Norwood. Please step up and take your Golden Kelly Award as a memory of that infamous day." The standing ovation and applause never seemed to end. "That does it for me. Next we have special events."

First up was Mayor Monroe. "As mentioned in that earth shattering letter, we the city council and the three other members in that letter are providing a quarterly subsidy to pay for local and panhandle people who cannot afford to pay for their care in the Polio Center including the breathing center, the observation rooms, and the in and outpatient rehab center. This first bank draft covers the last four months. We will continue this quarterly subsidy till the end of the polio epidemic." Angus McKenzie was quick to step up to accept the subsidy. Applause followed. The next to speak was a total unknown.

"Hello, my name is Sterling Cassidy and I am the CEO of Texas Mutual Insurance. We are the insurers of the King fairgrounds and its circus. Weeks ago I sent our adjuster to this hospital. The CEO wanted to offer us a simplified bill of days in the hospital with a fee for each operation and doctor's fees. My adjuster reacted on my orders and asked for a detailed accounting of every costs each patient incurred. Well we got the detailed bill. I looked at page one of 100 pages and found an aspirin charge of 3 cents each, a nickel for two, and a penny charge for each privacy paper used." Laughter broke out. "I won't bore you with any other charges and I turned to the 100th typed page and saw a total for each patient from the mass shooting including the outpatients treated in the ER—which we had forgotten. The bill was a shocker except for a preparation charge of $20. I told our CFO to pay the bill and add $80 to the preparation fee to cover our usual preparation fees of a dollar per page. So, here is the bank draft to cover for your excellent care. If we ever do business again we will accept your balanced bill of daily care plus surgeries and doctor fees." Mister Cassidy said thank you as Angus accepted the bank draft with a smile. Applause followed as Addie was seen clapping loudly.

Doctor Hallett introduced the next speaker. "This is Yvon Hasselbach of the March of Dimes." "Hello. As you know we provide all the orthotic braces and wheelchairs that your polio patients need on discharge—free of charge but we accept donations. As of today, we have reached an agreement with Mike Walters and any polio patient who needs a wooden lung at home will get one free of charge. The rotunda exploded with more applause and laughter.

Doctor Hallet then introduced the next speaker. "This next speaker is not offering any awards or money; but he has a lot to say! This is Doctor Carl Huxley, Director of medical and surgical training at the Dallas Medical Center." Doctor Huxley got to the podium and said, "I am proud to say that the Kelly Hospital medical staff of doctors are all graduates of our training program including the specialties of vascular, orthopedic, and urology." After a long applause the doc continued. "I remember each and everyone as if it was yesterday—especially that feisty wife of the soft-spoken Doctor Kelly." More laughter and applause. "I knew they would all succeed but not to this extent; anyways I am so very proud of you."

"Now the reason I am standing here is to inform you that neurosurgery is a fast-growing surgical specialty. As two of our graduates have done their first case, I am pleased to say that we have hired a renown US neurosurgeon from the Mass General Hospital. Plus his wife is a neurologist—a medical doctor that diagnoses brain diseases, treats them, or refers them to her husband for surgery. The current course for surgeons in our training program is two months long and the course repeats itself every two months. It includes classroom time from the neurosurgeon but emphasis is place on actual live surgery. I am extending a personal invitation to both Doctor James Kelly and Doctor Eric Hall to register for this program. As fast as this field is changing, the course might vary each year as new info and techniques come out."

"In the same light, the neurologist is also offering a two-month program of neurology for medical doctors. I am also extending an invitation to any medical doctor who wants to specialize but it is clear that a husband-and-wife team would seem to work out the best, heh? So Dottie and Susie, I also personally extend my invitation to become a certified neurologist. Thank you for your time." Applause followed.

Doctor Hallet got up and said, "Let's take a 15-minute break to stand, stretch, walk about, and use the facilities. We will then reconvene for the last two special awards—and the surprise reasons for this gathering."

*

"If you will all take your seats we will present the finale. The next to last award can only be presented by someone who has followed our awardee for the past 30 years. Of course I am referring to our generous philanthropist, Mister Gregory." To everyone's surprise the man got a standing ovation—clear proof that many attendees had benefited from his generosity. Mister Gregory started.

"Thank you for the invitation and greeting. Today I am fortunate to present an award that reflects a life's work and the recognition it deserves. Let me digress with a short but true story. 30 years ago I presented to your new hospital ER with a gut shot wound. Realizing that in 1905 that being gut shot was a death sentence; I asked for a bottle of laudanum, a quiet room, with a nurse at my side. The response was instant silence from the ER staff. All of a sudden a tall slim angelic blonde dressed in a white uniform sat by my side as she said, 'Mister Gregory, you don't have to die, we can save you!'"

"Well, needless to say that I had the operation. As I woke up from the anesthesia, I vividly saw the tall Doctor Kelly standing over me. Expecting the worse he said, 'I am sorry to say Mister Gregory, but you are going to have to live another 40 years!' To rub it in, Missus Kelly was standing by her husband with the biggest smile that clearly said, 'I told you so!' Proud as a peacock, I walked out of the hospital, sold my gold mine, and spent 30 years giving my wealth away. I may add that this hospital got very little of my wealth because the administrator wanted to pay their own way." The place erupted in laughter.

"Now getting back to the present, every successful organization seems to have a person who works from the sideline but manages to get things done. This person has shown innovation and astuteness to adapt to stressful times. Looking back this person started as a nurse and eventually became her husband's surgical assistant. When the need arose for someone to lead the hospital, this person took the reins."

"After going thru some thriving years, the wheels of progress came to an end when faced with WW1 and losing a surgeon to a front hospital in Europe. At the end of the war, the hospital was faced with dealing with the 1918 influenza. A special ward was created to treat the sickest influenza victims with dehydration and pneumonia. With the right staff, hundreds of patients made it home, thanks to this one person."

After the influenza epidemic, this person had a vision of how to save this hospital. She convinced three surgeons to go back to training and that resulted in the specialties mentioned. With a new method of advertising by newspapers, the county docs started sending their patients here for specialty care. After the prosperous years of the Roaring 20's, the market crashed and the Great Depression stressed the hospital to its maximum. Despite hard times a CODE D was established to handle a disaster. Every employee was assigned a position to immediately man when hearing the alarm for a CODE D. Then came the Polio epidemic."

"Without a second thought, this person worked with her daughter and daughter-in-law to establish a polio center. No one knows, but the Kellys used private funds to buy the first iron lungs and rocking beds." There was a pause and absolute silence as Addie was seen hiding her face. "Need I say more, this person has built this hospital and guided its survival thru several disasters. This person is a magnificent lady who now heads a major polio center to include a breathing room, observation rooms, an orthotics room, and an in and outpatient rehab center that serves this city, this panhandle 26 counties, and many adjoining communities." After another pause with total silence, Mister Gregory said, "ladies and gentlemen, doctors and nurses, without further ado, I present the amazing leader, Missus Adelle Kelly, better known as Addie." The place broke out in a roar which made the windows clatter. The applause was deafening and the only people still sitting were Brad and Addie. Brad was holding his wife while whispering private words in Addie's ear. Once the applause quieted down Mister Gregory said, "Doctor Kelly would you escort your lovely wife to the stage?"

When the Kellys arrived on stage, Mister Gregory gave Addie a hug as he whispered, "what will now happen is punishment for not taking more of my money over the 30 years." "Adelle Kelly, it gives me the greatest of pleasure to award you the Amarillo CEO of the year." More applause. Then the governor stepped forward.

"Missus Kelly, after reading that letter about your CODE D's response to a mass shooting, I wrote an executive order requiring all hospitals in Texas to immediately prepare a CODE D to mimic the one produced by Adelle Kelly CEO of the Kelly Hospital in Amarillo, Texas. The original affidavit is framed for you to display as you see fit." More applause as a crying Addie made her way back to her seat.

Once things settled down, Governor Rust stepped to the podium. "Now is the time to share with you why this event was set up. When I received this newspaper article about a CODE D response, I will admit that I reread it twice. I then assigned a staff member to investigate this local hospital. The result of the investigation was astonishing especially with what you have done with your polio center. Consequently I reviewed the application for Medical Center status that was included in the newspaper article as applied by the four men who wrote the article. I am now proud to say that for the first time in five years we have added a new medical center to our Texas medical system. That will allow this new medical center to receive its share of the state subsidy for advancing medical care in our state. Obviously, I am referring to this wonderful hospital which will now be called, 'The Kelly Medical Center of Amarillo, Texas.'"

*

The next morning, Benjamin True, Doctor Hallet, and the ten Country Doctors were invited to breakfast and for a fair on current medical equipment used in the breathing center. After the meal Dottie and Susie presented the new handheld breathing machine and the possibility of using a wooden lung on polio victims that were close to having respiratory failure.

The girls gave a demo. Dottie placed an airway in her mouth as Susie applied the face mask and squeezed the bag to inflate Dottie's chest. The first question was about that thing placed in Dottie's mouth. "That is an airway that keeps the tongue from being pushed down the throat during the bag squeezing and plugging the air passing to the lungs." After the demo it was made clear that an ambulance operator or train conductor could easily be trained to work the breathing bag and could accompany polio victims during their train ride to Amarillo.

The Country Docs were impressed and each paid $5 for both bag and airway as Addie would mail the unit once the local machine shop made them. Mister True then added that the railroad would pay for 50 of such units to be place on trains and controlled by the conductors. The next item was a discussion on the wooden lung. Dottie breached the subject and said, "why couldn't every railroad terminal have a wooden lung?" Doctor Hallet added, "it is a financial issue since many terminals are small and service only a few hundred locals." Susie added, "then why couldn't connecting terminals have at least one?" "Doctor Hallett paused and said, "yes that is possible. We have six connecting terminals plus the large community of Dumas. Seven units are a possibility as long as the conductors can train volunteers to manually operate the wooden lung."

Mister True added, "from what I now know, if we did have a wooden lung at the seven connecting terminals, we could easily save lives. Bottom line, we will split the bill if Doctor Hallet pays for his half." "I have the panhandle funds and will be glad to pay my half as long as you start training the conductors on both units, heh?" "Will issue the orders today!"

*

Over the next two weeks, referrals started coming in from those 10 county docs. Jimmy was spending time assisting his dad at performing vascular surgery as Eric was spending time with his dad doing non-invasive urological procedures with the cystoscope and the wire cutting resectoscope. It had been a month when a telegram came from Doctor Huxley. The team of Doctors Warren and Ida Mosher in neurology and neurosurgery were ready to offer their two-month course in Neurology and Neurosurgery after they trained the last class of medical and surgical residents. The subject was traumatic brain injuries, subarachnoid hemorrage, epidural and subdural hematomas, and brain tumors—how to diagnose and treat them medically or surgically.

Addie called an emergency meeting of the medical staff. There was a unanimous opinion that this hospital should add a Neurology and a Neurosurgical Department. The volunteers were the husband-and-wife teams of Doctor Jimmy and Susan Kelly and the other team of Doctor Eric and Dorothy Hall. Eric, with Dottie's approval, preferred to delay their neurological training so he could get more proficient at doing the transurethral prostate resection while Dottie would head the breathing center by herself.

No one knew that Dottie had a secondary motive for delaying her return to Dallas for more training. Everyone was aware that she had a major commitment in the breathing center. Despite being busy, once Jimmy and Susie would depart for Dallas, she was planning major meetings with Doctor Greene—the purpose being for adding another department to help save the hospital.

Fortunately referrals started coming in from the 10 country doctors that had been at the governor's meeting. It was Addie who realized that the 10 country doctors who had stayed on the job needed to see the Kelly Hospital, visit with the medical staff, and especially meet the new doctors on staff. Before Jimmy and Susie departed, she managed to arrange a welcome party for the leftover country docs. The visit lasted two days and the specialty surgeries were emphasized. The real clincher that made the visit successful was the fact that they were able to witness an endarterectomy, a TURP (transurethral resection of the prostate), and a hip fracture pinning.

*

On schedule, the second Duo made their way to Dallas. Registering with Doctor Huxley was a nostalgic event. After paying the two $1,000 fees, they were assigned to the couple's housing, given a triple meal tickets, and given two recently published textbooks—'Using the neuro exam to locate intracranial hematomas and surface brain tumors,' by Ida Mosher MD, and 'The surgical technique for evacuating intracranial hematomas and removing surface brain tumors,' by Warren Mosher MD.

The new Duo was torn between spending Friday at the pool versus starting to read the long-awaited textbooks. So they decided to start with the pool, followed by long overdue love making, and they would start reading come Saturday morning.

Getting up late from a busy night, they sat with their first cup of coffee as there was a knock at the door. Still barely clad, Susie threw a robe on and opened the door. An intra medical center messenger handed Susie a message and waited for an answer. Susie said "yes, we shall be there!"

Handing the message to Jimmy, he read:

From the desk of the Moshers,
Welcome. We hope you can join us by 3PM today for a social gathering followed by a Texas meal. An answer to the messenger will suffice. Warren and Ida Mosher, #39 Doctors Row c/o the Dallas Medical Center.

Again putting the textbooks aside, the new Duo jumped in the pool till 1PM when they had a lunch of soup and sandwich. By 3PM they were at the door of #39 Doctors Row. As the door opened, there stood the two Moshers with pleasant smiles and a warm welcome.

After small talk, Ida said, "Doctor Huxley has told us about you two, your parents, and that wonderful hospital in Amarillo. Warren then added, "so allow us to tell you about us. Because we were the children of college science professors, we easily entered John

Hopkins University in Baltimore, Maryland. We spent ten years there and the last two were spent in Neurology for Ida and Neurosurgery for me. After graduation we were wooded to join the staff at Mass General in Boston. After five years of clinical and research experience we were given an offer by Doctor Huxley that we could not refuse. So after six months of training surgical residents, we are ready to train outlying physicians the new division in medicine— neurology and neurosurgery."

Jimmy shocked them when he said, "now why would you do that; we would only become your competitors being only 300 miles from you in an 8-hour train ride?" Ida took over. "Because of the basic rule that says, 'see one, do one, and teach one.' Actually we have refined the saying because we feel blessed to have the perfect training that got us to Dallas, and we think that you two and your sister/ husband will be the new advanced educators." "What makes you think we will ever be part of a training center?" Warren smiled and added, "it is inevitable, all medical centers eventually add a teaching program from basic medical school to surgical training and beyond." "We know that the four of you have the mindset, the mental capability, and the surgical prowess to be brain surgeons or clinical neurologists."

The new Duo was pensive as Ida added, "Susie, I will hold a class every morning then I will do rounds on the new Neurology floor with you at my side. Afterwards we will do our daily admissions, and detailed physical exams. I guarantee you that at the end of the two months, you will be certified as a new Neurologist."

Warren then added, "I will not have classroom time. Neurosurgery is learned by doing it. I have an average of one open head operation each day and sometimes more. Even if it is not related to hematomas or brain tumors, it is related to doing brain surgery and you will be assisting me in all cases. Eventually, you will be doing most of the cases. That is how you will learn. So leave the diagnostic part to your wife and concentrate on the proper surgical technique."

"Finally, we have always believed that reading ahead promotes learning so that is why we have written the texts that you will use. We can only say that the students ahead of you all agreed that they were very helpful." "So what do you think, is this a go?" "Absolutely!" "Great, then let's eat. We have been smelling those Texas barbeque ribs since we awoke today."

**

CHAPTER 8

The New Specialties

Susie entered the classroom only to fine Ida at the front desk and at least a dozen medical students in attendance. Ida then added, "these are senior medical students who are auditing the class for their education, will not be graded, and will hold questions till the Q & A session. Have a seat and I will provide you with all you need to know about subdural hematomas commonly referred to as SDH."

"A subdural hematoma is a blood clot or liquid blood accumulation that forms between the membrane over the brain (dura) and the brain. It is usually caused by head trauma which can result in a skull fracture or can result in a blood vessel (artery or vein) tear under the dura with or without a skull fracture. So a skull fracture can be associated with a subdural hematoma or it may not."

"The major symptoms are a headache with increasing severity of a headache, and confusion with varying levels of consciousness. Plus any of the following:

Feel sick with dizziness, nausea, and vomiting.

Mental fog, memory loss, and personality change.

Fatigue and sleepiness.

Slurred speech.

Visual disturbances such as double vision or ptosis (drooping eyelid).

Unilateral paralysis or hemiparesis (weakness) contralateral to hematoma.

Unstable gait with or without falling.

Unilateral seizure ipsilateral to brain hematoma.

Elevated ICP (increased intracranial pressure)."

SDH--PHYSICAL FINDINGS ON NEURO EXAM.

"The initial exam is a baseline—any change is significant.

1. Eyes. Papilledema (swollen indistinct optic nerve) is diagnostic of increased intracranial pressure. Ptosis and paralyzed ocular muscles leading to double vision are all located in the occipital lobe behind the parietal lobe. Dilated or unreactive pupil is ipsilateral to the hematoma. It includes hemianopsia (loss of half of visual fields).

2. Sensory. Light touch, taste, and pain are all processed in the parietal lobe before transferred to the sensory cortex behind the motor cortex.

3. Reflexes. Normoactive and symmetric is the norm. Hyperreflexia or asymmetry is related to a hematoma as is ankle clonus or a positive Babinski sign. Usually contralateral to the hematoma.

4. Speech and aphasia is located in the left frontal lobe (Broca's area) and is on the same side as the hematoma.

5. Motor. Weakness or paralysis is contralateral to the hematoma.

6. Disorganized gait or poor balance is from the cerebellum and usually denotes a poor 'finger to nose test' or a poor gait with 'heel to toe gait.'

7. Facial appearance. Bilateral periorbital edema (coon's eyes) with or without otorrhea or rhinorrhea are usually caused by a basilar skull fracture with or without a SDH.

8. Mental status changes without other manifestations usually means the frontal cortex.

9. Temporal lobe hematomas lead to subtle findings of managing emotions, storing and retrieving memories, and understanding languages. This lobe is very sensitive to instigating seizures."

DIAGNOSTIC TESTING AND GENERAL DISCUSSION.

"A careful history of how the injury occurred plus the location of scalp bruising, bleeding, and scalp hematoma will usually locate a subdural hematoma.

Yet the use of skull X Rays to detect a skull fracture is diagnostic of the hematoma location. The use of a hyper penetrated frontal view can often show a midline shift of the calcified pineal gland to verify the presence of a hematoma. That, mixed with the neuro physical exam, will usually locate the subdural hematoma. Always remember, without a history of trauma be suspicious of dicumarol use as an anti-coagulant or the use of aspirin."

"Just remember these unique facts:

1. The greatest mimicry to a subdural hematoma is a brain tumor—especially the brain surface tumors.

2. Remember that a midline shift of 5mm or greater is a life-threatening event and as it means brain compression as seizures are common. Also, with elevated intracranial pressure (ICP), that brain herniation is possible before death.

3. In our time, a large subdural hematoma without surgery has a 90% mortality rate and with surgery it is down to 40-50% or less.

4. Forgotten symptoms of SDH are often mistaken for mental illness. Especially if accompanied with loss of speech, withdrawn behavior, apathy, blunted affect, and poor self-care and hygiene. That is where a careful neurological exam will detect the abnormalities of a SDH.

5. Very small hematomas are rarely treated surgically. Yet the accepted treatment is based on allowing the brain to recover electrically from the shocked brain. That means weeks to months of rest from physical activity, sports, work, or mental taxing. This includes good nutrition, no aspirin, and a gradual return to normal activities as long as the patient feels capable to do so."

SURGICAL TREATMENT.

"A craniotomy is the gold standard. The surgeon flaps the scalp on itself, removes a plate of skull, cuts the dura to allow a large suction tube to enter the hematoma and with plenty of saline irrigation sucks out the clots as pieces of clots and blood. He then sews the dura opening and replaces the skull plate and sutures the scalp back in place. Sometimes a small drainage tube is left in the hematoma space to drain late fluid accumulations or to detect a rebleed. Since I am not a practicing neurosurgeon I want you to take my synopsis and go in the viewing balcony and see my husband perform this procedure."

"That finishes my first lecture and we will hold questions for the later Q & A session. Tomorrow's class will cover traumatic brain injury (TBI), subarachnoid hemorrhage (SAH), and epidural hematoma (EDH). Reading ahead is recommended."

*

That same first morning, Jimmy was having coffee with Warren in the OR doctor's lounge. Warren said, "this is going to be a busy day. I have three cases that accumulated in the past week and weekend. We will start with a subdural hematoma that is about 10 days old and was the result of a heavy weight falling on top of the patient's head. So the hematoma is located over the occipital lobe with the patient presenting with multiple visual defects. The other two cases I will present each one during the interoperative rest periods as the OR team prepares the next case." "Do you have your own operating room?" "Yes, all specialty surgeries in this medical center have their own theatres because of the different equipment we need to do our work—besides, you wouldn't want to do a head operation when the room is full of plaster dust from a previous orthopedic case, heh?"

And so after a careful scrubbing, the operation started once the patient was under anesthesia. With a long scalp incision and extensive cautery of generous scalp bleeders, Warren formed a scalp flap and then retained the two folded edges with retractors. Using a special manual saw a skull plate was removed to expose the dura. Thru a short incision a small tube was inserted but no fluid was removed. In ten days, the blood had congealed into a true solid hematoma. The dura incision was extended to allow the entry of a larger suction catheter. With plenty of added saline and a vigorous breaking up of the hematoma, the foreign accumulation was removed. Once hemostasis was confirmed, the dura was sutured and the bony skull plate refitted into place. The scalp was returned to normal and cut ends sutured.

"The second case of the day arrived in our ER only two hours ago. The ER staff has just stabilized his vital signs from the extensive scalp damage from a gunshot wound. Our job is to explore the brain surface, cauterize bleeders with a low energy cautery, debride the compromised tissue, and remove the many bone fragments. Since most of the skull was blown away from a surface wound, we will have to place a stainless-steel plate and screws to secure the damaged bony plate area. This is not a very pretty operation, but with our violent land, it is one that frequently appears in our ER."

The operation started with extensive scalp debridement and sterilization. With the scalp flap in place, multiple bone shards and fragments were cleared away—a perfect nidus for infection. With the brain debridement and hemostasis completed, the dura was repaired and then a stainless-steel plate was applied but not secured in place. That would allow brain edema to lift the plate as the scalp was closed with removable clips. Warren then said, "once the brain edema has resolved we will open the scalp incision, secure the plate with stainless-steel screws, and suture the scalp closed. During the edema period, we will cover this patient with triple antibiotics, the best hyperosmolar IV solution we have for edema, barbiturate anticonvulsants, and hope for the best."

The last case of the day was a well followed patient in Ida's neurology clinic. "This man has had a progressive headache, mental fog and progressing confusion. With the headache being on the front left and the newly developing papilledema; we have no choice but to explore and find out if this is a brain tumor or what?"

The operation to reach the dura was uneventful. With a long incision the dura was entered and a moderate size surface tumor was visualized. Although it appeared to be a benign one, the key factor was whether it could be resected without much damage to the brain. After an hour of careful dissection, it was clear that there was little extension of the tumor into the deeper portions of the brain. After a long process of careful blunt dissection, the tumor was pulled thru the dura's incision. By the time the operation came to an end, the pathologist's frozen section was that it was malignant but the borders were all clear of the cancer cells.

Resting in the doctor's lounge with a fresh cut of coffee, Warren added, "we were lucky today as most malignant tumors cannot be resected because of deep extensions into the brain. In this case, we hope the oncologists have a post-surgical treatment plan of either radiation or the new chemotherapy agents that can cross the blood-brain barrier. So being about 5PM, we'll call it quits. We will meet at 8AM and start with post-op neurosurgical rounds. Tomorrow the early cases are from resident neurosurgical attendings doing carpal syndrome releases and peripheral nerve transpositions. Our first case will be at noon as we will start our rounds with this only neurosurgical case for tomorrow. Since your training does not include night or weekend work, then have a restful night. Reading ahead is to your benefit so include the subject of 'coup-contra-coup.'"

*

That evening, the new Duo met and went to the cafeteria for supper. Afterwards, they rushed to their apartment and quickly found themselves deeply involved in the new texts. Jimmy interrupted Susie by saying, "hey, we are still newlyweds and we should have jumped in the sac instead of putting our nose in the book." "Well I have three subjects to read and an hour will take care of my assignment" "Well, I only have one subject so what am I going to do till you are ready?" "Well, don't start without me, heh? Besides a short time waiting will pay off."

After a wild evening and night, the new Duo made it to breakfast by 7AM. Arriving at the neurology classroom, Ida started. "Today we will cover epidural hematomas (EDH), subarachnoid hemorrhages (SAH), and traumatic brain injuries (TBI)."

EPIDURAL HEMATOMAS.

"Unlike the SDH, this is the sudden accumulation of blood between the skull and the dura—instead of being between the dura and the brain as it is with a SDH. It is usually caused by trauma and often associated with a skull fracture and a tear in the dura over the fracture site. Although it can happen anywhere over the skull; since the skull is thinnest over the temples, this is usually where the hematoma develops."

"The clinical manifestation includes an initial loss of consciousness followed by a lucid period, and then a sudden crashing of the patient into unconsciousness, usually associated with seizures, and profound bradycardia of the heart or elevated blood pressure or both."

"Let's not beat about the bush. This is a neurosurgical emergency and your job ends when you have made the diagnosis in conjunction with the neurosurgeon. Now there is a case heading for the OR as we speak and I am certain that your husband will discuss the emergency's definitive treatment. The reality is that without surgery, the mortality is high at 90%. With immediate evacuation of the hematoma thru Burr holes, and the definitive open repair of the dura, the survival rate is close to 75% and with half without residual."

"So we are left with the two medical management intracranial disorders. Let us begin with the dreaded subarachnoid bleed."

SUBARACHNOID HEMORRHAGE (SAH).

"This is free flowing blood mixing with the cerebrospinal fluid over the brain and spinal cord. Although it can result from trauma, nearly 95% of cases are spontaneous, and caused by a bleeding artery aneurysm (98%) or a rare congenital AV malformation. For all intended purposes this is a nonsurgical event."

"The ultimate diagnostic test is a spinal tap. If the fluid is bloody in all three collected tubes, the diagnosis is clear and releases the neurosurgeon. Sometimes the red cell count is done in all three tubes and a similar count is proof of a SAH."

"The symptoms of a SAH are as follows:

1. A sudden explosive headache like one that the patient has never experienced.
2. Stiff neck.
3. Nausea and vomiting.
4. Blurred or double vision.
5. Altered level of consciousness or seizures
6. Stroke symptoms with speech and or hemiparesis.
7. High blood pressure which only makes the bleeding worse!
8. For elevated intracranial pressure manifested as papilledema, a small tube is inserted thru burr holes to release some excess fluid as hyperosmolar infusions are also used to minimize brain edema."

"Other than barbiturate anticonvulsants, morphine provides the best sedation and headache pain relief. Waiting conservatively, things get complicated if there is a rebleed or secondary vasospasm which cause a host of new worrisome neurological symptoms that tend to be temporary. And always be alert of patients on dicumarol of self-treating with aspirin. Be very attentive of a patient's blood pressure since a high pressure will certainly cause a rebleed or vasospasm. In closing, I may add that aneurysm clipping is a research project on the east coast major neurosurgical centers. It is possible that your husband might be involved with such treatments, if and only if, we have intracranial and arterial imaging to locate the bleeding aneurysms. I am certain that it might be the subject of discussion at your apartment tonight, heh?" "Oh I am sure of it!" "The last subject is the new nomenclature for getting knocked out, traumatic brain injury (TBI)."

TRAUMATIC BRAIN INJURY.

"A concussion is the correct term for losing consciousness from trauma. Whether it is short or long in duration it is still a concussion. That means that the shockwave from the trauma has disrupted the brain's electrical activity. Until the electrical activity returns, coma will continue.

Clinically we now classify these brain injuries as mild, moderate, and severe because of the differing managements. Although usually asymptomatic, symptoms can include: Increasing headache, poor coordination, nausea and vomiting, sleepiness to unresponsive sleep, visual disturbances, unilateral or bilateral dilated pupils, slurred speech, seizures and the common amnesia of the event. These symptoms run the gamut of mild to severe as coma or seizures are the most alarming symptoms that need advanced medical care."

Basically, the treatment is no work, add peace and quiet, good nutrition, and plenty of rest from anywhere between one month for the mild cases and three months for the severe cases. I have always said that all concussions should start their treatment by booking in the Dallas Queen Hotel, use and sit by the heated pool, enjoy three meals a day, take two naps a day, and flounder away the week without even reading to tax your brain. But I know that is unrealistic."

"Keep in mind that the brain needs time to resume normal electrical activity. The trauma has damaged neural cells and pathways that have to be replaced by new cells and pathways. That takes time, and if the brain is taxed prematurely it will likely malfunction for unknow periods of time. So the bottom line is if a patient has rested and feels able to return to work, it is probably time to let him or her among the working class—especially if a gradual return to work program is available."

"That does it for this morning. Tonight's assignment is to read the section on coup-contra-coup brain injuries. Next, you and I will do rounds on the neurology ward and the rest of the auditing class is dismissed."

*

Jimmy had just poured another cup of coffee while waiting for Warren in the doctor's OR lounge when the door slammed open and Warren said, "Jimmy quickly follow me, we have a neurosurgical emergency in the ER!"

While almost running to the ER Warren said, ;I know we were to discuss and operate on a case of coup-contra-coup, but that can wait till noon or later. What we have now needs to be acted on immediately and we may not see another case for weeks from now."

On arrival, a young man was having a right sided seizure and was comatose. He had a bruise and laceration on his left temple from a whiskey broken bottle in a barroom fight. Warren started giving orders, "Jimmy prep the scalp over the laceration, make a two-inch incision, separate the scalp edges with the self-retaining retractors. I'll get the burr hole saw ready for this is an epidural hematoma that needs to be drained now or we'll lose this young man."

Warren kept the saw rolling till a ¾ inch bone plug was removed as a jet of blood erupted from the burr hole and splattered all over Warren's scrubs. The entire ER staff 'oohed and aahed' in surprise. Warren then asked Jimmy to insert a suction catheter into the bloody cavity. With blood and clots removed, Jimmy could still see bright red arterial blood accumulating in the cavity. Warren then said, "we have an arterial bleeder that needs to be tied off. That means exploratory surgery till we find it." Looking at the ER head nurse he said, "notify the OR supervisor that we are on our way and need a room STAT to do an epidural exploration." Leaving the suction catheter to gravity drainage, the orderly started moving the patient to the OR as the two neurosurgeons went to scrub up.

The scalp incision was extended and a 2-inch by 3-inch bone plate was removed. The dura was carefully examined and a good-sized artery was seen pumping away. After cauterizing the tip and tying a suture for good measure, the two bone plates replaced, and the scalp sutured. With the epidural space now empty, the compressed brain would resume its normal shape and position. Otherwise, it was a matter of time to see if the patient would wake up. As empiric management, IVs were maintained, Oxygen kept on the patient, and an anti-convulsant maintained prophylactically.

With the procedure finished, the neurosurgical OR was given to the other neurosurgeons doing their peripheral nerve procedures, as Warren and Jimmy went to do their daily rounds on the neurosurgical ward.

*

The next day, Ida started class with the words, 'coup-contra-coup' or the modern version 'coup-contrecoup.' "This is the great masquerader of hidden brain dysfunction, brain bruising, and in the extreme as one or two subdural hematomas. So in its mild form it is a medical management event and in its extreme a neurosurgical event. As a definition, the coup is the impact of the brain against the skull as the 'contrecoup' is the injury that takes place on the opposite side of the skull from the original impact. To simplify, it is a 'whiplash' that is the characteristic injury as the 'contrecoup' usually causes more brain trauma than the 'coup.'"

"Pretend being in a car as the vehicle abruptly stops on a tree. The body stops but the brain continues sliding forward as it stops against the skull (coup). Actually the brain bounces back and then comes in contact with the back of the skull (the more serious contrecoup). In both instances the brain gets bruised, develops edema, bleeds, and can form a hematoma. The severe cases involve the catastrophic intracerebral bleeds."

"Since most of these injuries are asymptomatic, it is easy to see why they are often not treated. At other times there are symptoms and the most common are: headache or increasing headache, fatigue, visual defects, poor balance, confusion, dizziness, insomnia. It is possible that any coup-contrecoup injury can lead to seizures, hematomas, or even death. There are three unusual things that are worth mentioning.

1. It also seems that we are seeing the elderly fall and hit the back of their heads—making it the common cause for such an injury."

2. The loss of smell and taste is a common finding with what even appears to be an insignificant injury.

3. An axonal injury is the most serious of coup-contrecoup injuries. This occurs when the brain is shaken or twisted because that causes

a tear of connecting fibers called axons. This is often a fatal event."

"I had a case of coup-contrecoup that I was watching in the neurology ward. Because his symptoms worsened he was transferred to Warren's ward and is scheduled for a bilateral exploration. I am sure you will hear all about it tonight. Anyways, if you have time read ahead on tomorrow's subject—Parkinsons disease."

*

That night, Susie had started her monthly. So Jimmy went to bed early to catch up on sleep. Susie, who had observed several Parkinsons patients in Ida's ward, got involved in reading about the disease. After reading excerpts from three texts, Susie was certain that Ida would know more than what was in the published texts.

The next morning, the new Duo was ready for more learning experiences. Jimmy was next with an early case. Warren started saying, "this is a classic case of extreme 'whiplash' or 'coup-contrecoup.' The man was rearended at 25 mph while waiting at a stop sign." "Yes, I reviewed the case after rounds yesterday." "Good, then tell me, since we are doing a double exploration, are we going to find the most pathology from the frontal lobe or the rear occipital and cerebellar lobes?"

"Well, I agree that he has cerebellar ataxia but it actually looks like he is walking like a bowlegged cowboy that spends all day in the saddle. Whereas his frontal cortex is so affected that he has no idea whether he is 'afoot or on horseback.' Now I know that Ida and Suzie can describe his neurological defects in technical terms, but as a surgeon I rely on what the patient does or looks like. In that light the frontal lobe will be the lobe most affected and probably has a hematoma—and I am sticking to my assessment till I am vindicated or reprimanded, heh?" Warren laughed till both surgeons were gowned and gloved ready for surgery.

Once the operation was started, both the frontal lobe area and the cerebellar/occipital areas were prepped. Warren made the decision to explore the frontal area first—based on Jimmy's gut feeling and his rationale that not knowing if a person was 'afoot or horseback' was a more relevant issue than walking like a bowlegged cowboy. The burr hole exploration revealed an intact dura but thru an incision was found a sizeable subdural hematoma. Once the operation was done, Warren decided to hold on exploring the posterior skull for the time being—pending how the patient's gait would progress. Afterwards, the surgeons did rounds and prepared for tomorrow's operations.

*

Meanwhile, Ida started her class on Parkinsons disease. "Parkinsons has been around over a hundred years as it was first described by a Doctor Parkinson as a neurological disorder first called, 'paralysis agitans.' Today there is definitely a new peak of occurrence as it has been postulated that it is related to the 1918 Influenza but proof is still pending. Anyways we have to deal with this disease as we know it and with the treatment we currently have."

"Parkinsons is a disease caused by a loss of brain cells that make dopamine—a chemical used to carry electrical activity signals between cells and pathways that control movement and coordination. With that said, the salient symptoms are:

1. Resting tremor that is often referred to as a pin rolling tremor.
2. General slowness called bradykinesis.
3. Stiff joints, shuffling gait, and cogwheeling joints.
4. Bland or sad facial expression.
5. Difficulty swallowing.
6. Generally unstable standing and walking—so easy to fall and result in skull or long bone fractures.
7. Slow speech.
8. Dementia—usually late in the disease and often fatal."

1940's Early Treatments. "The obvious answer is to produce dopamine or a precursor to dopamine. But these do not yet exist. So until they are available, we use current drugs that mimic dopamine, and are called 'dopamine agonists,' These drugs fall in the class called 'anticholinergics,' and include the following: belladonna alkaloids, drugs with ergot activity, and antihistamines such as the newly discovered phen-benzamine (Antergan), or diphenhydramine (Benadryl). There are two other classes of drugs that are direct dopamine agonists and those include bromocriptine and amphetamines."

"With all that in mind, it is time we discuss what new rules, we as clinicians, must learn to live with. The FDA (Federal Drug Administration) now requires that new drugs be 'shown safe' before marketing them to physicians or patients. So the old days of following researchers and trying new drugs, as long as the local pharmacists could find some, are gone. The problem is like any bureaucracy, the wheels turn slowly. You will often find widespread use of a new drug with excellent results even before it is on the docket for FDA review. This all means that the patient's welfare has to come first. If you and your patient are willing to take some informed risks, no one will stop you."

"And so that finishes today's lecture. For your benefit, I invite the auditing students to accompany Doctor Kelly and I on rounds so we can demonstrate the differing presentations of Parkinsons."

*

The intensive training continued for weeks. Suzie was spending all her time working the neurology ward. She spent many hours in the medical library reading about the many neurological diseases. Every day at 3:30PM she met with Ida to discuss one of the neurological disease that she had evaluated clinically and read what was available in the medical literature. In addition, she became very secure doing her detailed neurological exam on patients. The majority of admissions were those with complaints of headaches, confusion, hemiparesis, elevated intracranial pressure, and a myriad of other complaints and findings— all consistent with brain tumors. The neurologist's job was to use the history and neuro exam findings to locate the tumor to allow the neurosurgeons an entry port to expose the presumed brain tumor. That was how it was done when brain imaging was still unavailable.

Meanwhile, Jimmy was operating on at least one case each day. The hematomas were rare despite the Dallas Medical Center's catchment area of 360 degrees and with a radius of 150 miles. The unexplained fact was that there was a high incidence of brain tumors of which 50% were benign or malignant. Fortunately the benign ones could be resected 80-90% of the time whereas the malignant ones could be resected some 20-30% of the time—always depending on the time between onset of symptoms and exploratory surgery.

Yes, it was exploratory surgery at the recommendation of the neurologist. Most of the time the neurologists were correct in their diagnosis and location; but were never able to determine whether the lesion would be positive or negative for malignancy— that was Doctor Greene's job in reviewing a frozen section of the open biopsy.

Jimmy was a good learner and had fantastic surgical hands. At the start of the second month, Warren announced that he would become the surgical assistant and Doctor Kelly would now be the surgeon of record. This continued until the sad day when Jimmy and Suzie were handed their certificate—a certified Neurologist and Neurosurgeon.

*

The reunion back in Amarillo was a joyous event. It was Dottie who surprised everyone, including mom and dad. There was no doubt that maintaining 24 active polio cases, going thru the initial two weeks, then weaning, and finally getting training to properly use their braces was an exhausting commitment. Fortunately doctors Reinhart and Tisdale were spending the same hours as Dottie to watch over the patients in the iron or wooden lungs. Despite all this work, she admitted that she had time to plan for the future. "Doctor Greene and I see this hospital adding another specialty other than Neurology and Neurosurgery. It is time we treat our own cancer patients and stop referring them to Dallas. So, Daniel is leaving tomorrow for Dallas. He has registered for a 2-week course to get him started doing radiation therapy. Once he returns and gets the equipment added to the Xray department, he will return to training as new things come out. So, to compliment radiation therapy, I will split my two months in Dallas. One month to learn the neuro exam and interpretation of its meaning, and one month in Oncology to learn the new chemotherapeutic drugs coming out in the 40s and learn which ones to use for the specific malignancies—if one could be used with documented efficacy without horrendous side effects. I may add that I have been in contact with the head of Oncology, a Doctor Herman Nichols, and he is interested in traveling to our hospital one day a week to consult on the new patients who need a chemotherapeutic agent, and the ones already on treatments that I would be closely following—for a consultative fee of course."

Addie could not resist saying and asking. "Why would such a trained doctor put himself to such extra tiring work and travel?" "Simple, he has two kids ready for college and the salary of a medical training center staff does not cover college fees, and this doctor is in charge of a new group of doctors who believe that it is time for Dallas to farm out its specialist to outlying hospitals—to establish satellite offices and stop competing with hospitals the size of ours but to work with them."

"So as soon as Doctor Greene returns, hopefully with radiation equipment, Eric and I will leave for our turn in post graduate training. Oh before I forget, you and I will be taking over most of Doctor Greene's duties during his absence—except pathology, heh?"

**

CHAPTER 9

The Hospital Steward

Doctor Greene turned his two-week course into a 4-week training program. By the time he arrived, his radiation equipment was waiting for him. With the blueprints in his hands, the Walters team went to work expanding the Xray department with more lead lined walls.

The new second Duo arrived at their alma mater and after a nostalgic reunion with Doctor Huxley, they immediately went to work. Dottie was an eager learner, enjoyed Ida's early lectures, and was totally involved in following the patients in the neurology ward. Eric was in heaven assisting Warren. Each evening after supper at the cafeteria, the Duo was faithful in reading ahead the texts published by Ida and Warren, as well as many east coast neurological research centers. Like Jimmy and Susie, the new Duo was registered to receive several medical letters on all new drugs approved by the FDA, especially in neurology and neurosurgery. In the same line as Jimmy and Susie, they were receiving research experiments from the east coast large neuro-surgical centers.

The first month passed quickly as Dottie moved laterally into the Oncology department. Doctor Nichols was a charismatic speaker full of knowledge and enjoyed sharing with Dottie his accumulated facts on the new drugs being used to treat cancer— the blood malignancies and the solid tumors. Dottie specifically recalled his first class when Doctor Nichols said, "new drug development has finally changed from a low budget government research effort to an aggressive modern capitalistic system of privately funded research for a multimillion-dollar industry. You will find out that new drugs are coming out every day in multiple fields and especially in cancer and cardiology—the two major killers in this country."

After introductions, he laid out his training program. "I start each morning at 9AM with a presentation of a drug. I go over side effects in general, administration frequency, dosage, complications, the cancers that respond to this anticancer drug, and the % efficacy. In the late morning we do hospital rounds to care for the very ill with cancer. In the afternoon I run office hours seeing new patients and following up on those being treated or had treatment for cancer."

"Office hours generally finish by 3:30PM and we then have a discussion about the patients we saw today. That brings us to the time that Eric gets out of neurosurgery, as we meet at the cafeteria for supper. After supper we stop at the medical library and pick up texts appropriate for our current study."

Dottie was impressed hearing Herman's first lecture on 'nitrogen mustard.' "Nitrogen mustard is a cytotoxic alkylating agent that attacks the nucleus of dividing cells. It also is very toxic to the host who has the malignancy. Routine side effects include severe allergic reactions and bone marrow suppression. The latter, often within a week, leads to anemia, bleeding, a very high risk of infections, bloody diarrhea, hair loss, poor appetite, and a metallic taste in the mouth; just to name a few."

"Yet it has a profound effect on lymphoid and myeloid tissues and for this reason it is the number one drug used to treat lymphomas. There are several companies that make this drug under their own brand name. As of late, there are several reports of its beneficial effect on solid tumors as we will discuss each one in the future weeks."

"An important point to make is tumor access to any drug. If a cancer can be reached thru the circulatory system, the drugs will likely have an effect on it including the solid tumors. The problem with the brain is the 'blood brain barrier;' a poorly understood barrier that prevents many chemotherapeutic agents from ever passing thru; to flow in the circulatory system of the brain. Now, for neurosurgeons, this toxic drug is a miracle since it can easily pass thru this barrier and enter tumors of the brain—especially the ones that cannot be surgically resected. At times the surgeons can remove the bulk of a brain tumor with minimal extensions that were not removable. That is where nitrogen mustard comes to play along with radiation therapy. So remember the rule about brain cancerous tumors. The neurosurgeons make the diagnosis and do the surgery if possible. Then the oncologist along with the radiation therapist provide their contribution either as a combined or a single therapy."

The second lecture was about agents that were used against leukemia. Dottie was introduced to the anti-folate drugs against acute lymphocytic leukemia in children and adults. Later its use extended to other cancers, the first of which was for oral cancer. The real surprise of the day was the recent research on a drug called methotrexate which was showing great results against breast cancer. However by the end of the lecture Herman reminded Dottie, "as of today, there is not much that chemotherapy can do for pancreatic cancer, metastatic liver cancer, colon cancer, or lung cancers—the four lethal malignancies that are still a death sentence."

When the lecture series came to an end, Dottie was directed to the basic neurological exam to detect the location of presumed tumors. It quickly became clear that would be part of her job as the cancer specialist to help locate the brain tumors till brain imaging came along—for it would be her husband who would do the exploratory surgery.

Dottie delved into the chemo drugs available and which ones had documented positive results. Despite her knowledge, she was no match for Herman. That is when she had the brainstorm that led to a discussion of establishing a satellite oncology clinic at the Kelly Medical Center. To her surprise, he was more than interested. The fixed low income of a teaching professor was not conducive for two boys going to college. The reality was that Herman was offered a consultative fee for each patient he saw and advised Dottie to proceed with a certain chemo agent. The hook was set when Dottie said, "My mom, the hospital administrator, will add all your consultative fees for the day and before you take the train home you will have a bank draft from us—that's immediate payment and the hospital will wait the payment in due time—Amarillo time, heh?" It was the offer of a lifetime as he would be proud to oversee an amazing physician administer the chemotherapy agents during his absence.

So after the two months passed, the new Duo was on their way back home. Little did they know what Addie was planning. As the 'hospital steward,' she was going to use the new specialties to rejuvenate the referring physician program and put the medical center back in the black.

*

It was a special hot tub meeting when Addie said, "you may not have realized it, but I have been working on a plan to rejuvenate the physician referral program for specialty surgery. The reality is that we now have two medical programs that can be used for referral— the polio department, the new neurology department, as well as the new neurosurgery department—plus all the new things in vascular, orthopedics, urology, and the oncology department of the future."

Brad then added, "well tell me what this marketing plan is all about!" "It basically reverses the easy route—'out of sight, out of mind.' Neighboring country docs need to be reminded that we offer modern services and they need to feel that they are part of the team. So I have prepared an educational program to take care of the 'out of sight, out of mind' problem and one program to include all referring docs as part of our medical center. Let me outline the educational program."

"First we invite the panhandle docs that did not come to the governor's gala event. Plus we also invite the docs within our 150-200- mile catchment area. That includes up to Santa Rosa NM, Trinidad CO, Elk City OK, and Lubbock Tx. The day's events will include a morning tour of the hospital and a detailed tour of the breathing and rehab center. After lunch we will have short presentations from each surgeon and his specialty, as well as Suzie discussing the new neurology department. We will not yet mention the Oncology department or the Radiation department except to say that they are in the planning stages."

Brad had been very attentive when he added, "these docs are hard to move out of their niches. You need a dangling carrot to get them here." "I agree, so we include a refund for the train tickets, put them up in a hotel, provide all meals either in the hospital or hotel restaurant and even pay for miscellaneous personal expenses. They all need to see it as a paid holiday for overworked docs and a chance to meet our docs face to face."

Brad then added, "good, I like it, but isn't this a stop gap event. What can we add to attract all docs to this medical center?" "We start a monthly regular day for all outlying docs. The first will be an all-day affair to discuss SDH, brain tumors, and gunshot wounds to the head. That means that Jimmy and Eric will lead the day's event."

"That sounds great, so what do you have in store for the second month?" "The country docs were never exposed to the value of a detailed neuro exam or how to properly perform it. The girls will take turns in presenting the different aspects of the exam and how to use the findings to confirm a suspected brain tumor or a SDH. I am certain that this will take all day and should attract a high attendance."

Brad kept pushing, "so what is in store for the third month. "Introducing our medical center as a cancer treatment center. Doc Greene will explain how radiation works and will tour the new radiation treatment center. Then Doc Nichols will be here to introduce the new revolutionary chemotherapeutic approach to cancer. He can present the three chemotherapeutic agents we have and how they can affect tumor growth. Dottie will then explain the weekly consultation from the outside expert as she will head the treatment center during the following week."

"The fourth week, I think we should have a review of vascular, orthopedic, and urology. The new techniques and new equipment is what is keeping your good results and this needs to be shared with the referring doctors."

Brad was pensive as he finally said, "that is a good four-month plan, but what do we do after the four months? Do we repeat the entire program?" "NO, it is time to keep the docs informed of new drugs, treatments, or even surgical results. I am talking of a biweekly letter to all docs in our 150-mile catchment area." "And who is going to write it?" "Why me of course, but with input from every doc on staff. I even suspect that a report on recently FDA approved drugs will become the most important feature in the letter." "What will you call it?" "Why 'The Kelly Medical Center Medical Letter,' heh?"

Brad was pensive and finally admitted, "there is no doubt that marketing is the way to keep this hospital afloat, but as long as we do it professionally and never 'toot our horn.' For past experiences confirm that the squeaky wheel will get the grease, heh?" "For sure!"

After another pause, Brad added, "that was a long business meeting and every protruding part is getting puckered/prunished to include toes, fingers, and ..." "Not to worry, I know what to do to refill those parts. But bear with me, I only have one other issue to discuss." "Ok." "Pretend you are a country doc and you just sent one of your patients for a surgical procedure. What would irk you and what would please you?"

"I would be irked and insulted to not receive any communications from the doc at KMC till the patient returned home and gave me a prescription pad size note that said, Diagnosis, Treatment, Complications, and Discharge meds. How demeaning and patronizing." "Then tell me what would be an acceptable procedure that would inform you and give you the feeling that you are part of the team that cares for this patient."

Brad paused and then finally said, "I would be honored if I received an early telegram that included:

RE: PATIENT'S NAME

THANK YOU FOR THE REFERRAL STOP

AGREE WITH YOUR DIAGNOSIS OF COMMON DUCT OBSTRUCTION STOP

WILL PERFORM A CHOLECYSTECTOMY AND COMMON DUCT EXPLORATION STOP

PROGRESS TO FOLLOW STOP

BRAD KELLY MD

"Ok, well that can be a form telegram with embellishment, so what would you add as progress?" "Assuming that the post-op care was unremarkable, I would send a discharge telegram that said:

RE: PATIENT'S NAME

OPERATION UNEVENTFUL STOP

POST-OP CARE WITHOUT COMPLICATIONS STOP

DISCHARGE MEDS INCLUDE ... STOP

PATIENT TO SEE YOU WITHIN A WEEK STOP

PATIENT WILL CARRY OFFICIAL TYPED DISCHARGE SUMMARY AND MEDICATION INFO SHEET STOP

THANK YOU FOR INCLUDING US IN THE CARE OF THIS PATIENT STOP

BRAD KELLY MD

Addie smiled as she said, "that is informative, courteous, and somewhat diplomatic. I guess you are learning that it is easier to attract flies with molasses than vinegar, heh?" "Not really, it is however all about being respectful of other people—that includes the patients and the referring docs. Now how were you to reinflate my puckered tips?"

*

For the next week, Addie did what she did best. Talking with each medical staff doctor about her marketing plan and getting the guarantee that each doctor would comply with the two telegrams and a typed discharge summary (handwritten by the doc and typed by Addie). Addie knew that as a group at a medical staff meeting, the results were never guaranteed, but giving their word to Addie was sacred. It was no surprise that there was a unanimous vote to proceed with a very aggressive and costly marketing plan.

Looking back some four months, it was a major endeavor to invite the docs, pay for their expenses, and get the staff docs to prepare a day long lecture and demo workshop. What was the most shocking of all was that there was a direct correlation between the topics presented and to the referrals from the attending country docs.

The fifth month was a boom town at the Kelly Medical Center. The ORs were full from 8AM to 5PM and sometimes later. Addie could not keep up typing discharge summaries and running back and forth to the telegraph office. One fine morning she refused to get out of bed as she said to Brad, "I need a secretary to type these summaries and run to the telegraph office. So I am going to the local business college and will come back with a secretary."

Meanwhile Addie did a detailed review and found that the early statistics showed a clear peak in three areas of patient care—TURP and the associated local prostate cancer treatment, brain tumors, and the management of Parkinsons disease. What no one had anticipated was Doctor Nichols revelation. If a tumor is malignant but cannot all be removed, at least remove the bulk that is fairly safe and leave the smaller portions intact. He convinced Jimmy and Eric that debulking a malignant brain tumor allowed the combined radiation and chemotherapy agents a chance to control the tumor's growth— especially using the drugs known to cross the blood brain barrier. That quickly drove Doc Greene back to Dallas to learn the techniques and limitations in treating localized residual of malignant brain tumors.

*

Many months went by as the hospital census was kept at 150% occupancy. It was another of those infamous days when Addie called Brad into her office. "My darling husband, we have a problem. I have telegrams that say we have three major referrals each day for the next week. Where are we going to put them or do we delay the referrals?"

"We never delay referrals. So double up the rooms with two patients." "We did that two months ago!" "Close the observation rooms in the Polio Center and convert it to a post-op and Neurology ward." "We can do that but that will only give us a dozen more beds by doubling up." "Great, so problem solved, heh?" "Not by a long shot, the pharmacy is too small and many meds are kept unlocked in central supply, the OR is too small and we need three or four ORs, we need a separate neurology ward, a separate oncology ward, and more wards for post-op patients. Plus we need an auditorium as a gathering place, the radiation department needs more room and we need …"

"Enough, the writing is on the wall. Call Mike Walters and let's build an extension." "You know that there is no more room for another extension. He has told us that the next extension will be an attached self- standing structure with the potential for several floors high. The first floor would be for ancillary services as the second floor or higher would be for patient care." "I know, so let's do it. Doctor Hallet and Mister Gregory had said years ago that the need would eventually come to pass. Well our marketing has been successful and it is time to pay the price, heh?"

*

The next morning Addie called the Abernathy Architectural Associates. Aloysius, who had designed the last renovation and expansion, had retired. His son, Sean, had taken over the business and would be over this afternoon.

After introductions and pleasantries, Sean said, "I took the time to review my dad's old blueprint of your last expansion. He has a notation that the next expansion should be a separate multistory structure. Are you Ok with that?" "Yes, and this is what we want on the first floor:

1. Administrator's triple office—one for me, one for my husband, and one for our secretary.
2. Adjoining meeting/conference room for thirty or more medical staff.
3. A new X ray department for in and out-patients and a separate new radiation department.
4. A new accounting department for three or more employees with a private office for the CFO.
5. A secure pharmacy three times the original size
6. An auditorium for 200 people.

7. At the farthest end, a new central supply three times the original size with an outside unloading dock.

8. Include a new nursing office, conference room, and with a secretarial office.

Sean added, "what do we do with any leftover footage?" "Leave unfinished but enclosed till we find some use for it." "Out of curiosity, what will you do with the empty spaces around the rotunda?" "The pharmacy, administrative offices, nursing office, and accounting office will all be converted to new physician offices with treatment rooms and an expansion of the waiting room—especially the new visiting physician satellite from Dallas. The old Xray/radiation center will allow for a needed laboratory expansion. The old OR will be converted into patient rooms as the new OR with four operating rooms will be as the elevators open to the second floor."

Sean added, "other than the new OR suites, what will the 2nd floor be used for?" "Large patient rooms which can be converted into double occupancy when needed. It will be for the new neurology, neurosurgery, cancer patients, and the old vascular surgery." "Did you forget the old central supply?" "No, we'll expand the kitchen, cafeteria, and public bathrooms." "Any other plans?" "Yes, we'll get Mike Walters to do a complete facelift to the maternity ward and nursery. It is way overdue since it has the original décor."

An hour later, Sean and his team were ready to do their presentation. "In order to accommodate your first-floor design, we will need a building 40 X 200 feet—8,000 square feet. In this era, that will cost you $2 a square foot for the first floor and $1.50 a square foot for each additional floor. It will also include a brick building and a flat tarred roof to allow another floor in the future. Actually this structure is designed to have a total of four floors. My team and I will start working on blueprints and should have two copies within a week. I suggest you contact Mike Walters since we don't know what can happen with this war in Europe."

*

Mike Walters went over the details and confirmed the basic costs of goods in April of 1941. Mike was clear, "we need to put an order for thousands of bricks as early as tomorrow. We then take a week to place orders for everything else to cover the two floors. To cover 40 feet wide and multiple floors we are going to need at least three 41-foot-long I-beams to support up to three floors above the ground concrete floor— and that is with two supporting posts per I-beam and wooden beams in-between the steel I-beams. I-beams are still available, but if the US goes to war, the steel will be used to build ships and submarines. So I will also place the order for the three I-beams by morning. Call me when the blueprints arrive so I can go over them with you and the architect."

Four days later, Sean arrived as Mike was called in. Sheets and sheets of blueprints were examined as changes were made. Six hours later the team approved the final changes. Mike started work the next day to dig out the footing that could hold four floors. There was an unmentioned haste in the air as Mike added more construction carpenters, brick layers, finish carpenters, electricians, and plumbers. When confronted by Addie and Brad, Mike quickly answered, "war is coming and we need to be done this project no later than mid-October—or it will remain unfinished till the end of WWII."

It was October 15 when the grand opening was celebrated. Tours were open to the public to include the new building with elevators as well as the interior changes to include the maternity ward's cosmetic facelift.

*

Only two months passed before the inevitable occurred. Japan attacked Pearl Harbor and Hitler was ravaging Europe by invading one country after another. War was declared against Japan and Germany by the US Congress at President Roosevelt's request.

The draft had started a year before war was declared. It included single men between 21 and 35 as well as doctors up to age 45. It was no surprise receiving an official document that stated, "as hospital administrators, your presence is required at the local draft board hearing for next Wednesday. Bring list of all ages of single men between 21-35 and all male doctors, married or single, under age 45."

The Duo had four days to prepare their meeting with the draft board. The issue that needed reconciling was whether to fight inscription or to go along and lose two new doctors and up to ten single men. The Duo discussed the issues each night in their hot bathtub and did finally accept an approach that they considered best for all concerned.

The Duo was greeted by the aging Mayor Monroe. "Thank you for your punctuality. Before we enter the board's quarters, keep in mind that these are appointed civil authority workers whose job is to fill the ranks and deal with draft dodgers. They may sound cold with their words but it is their job. I can only say that they follow the written law." Addie looked at the mayor and added, "that is exactly what we will do—follow the written law! heh?"

After the mayor made introductions, the board's president started. "We have been assigned the task of in-scripting your young male workers and two surgical doctors from your Kelly Memorial Hospital. Do you have the list of names for those two categories?" "Yes but you are not getting it because we have a legal grievance." "Well it had better be good because we can send you to jail for interference in the legal inscription law."

Addie stood and said, "by order of our Texas Governor Rust, we are no longer the Kelly Memorial Hospital, but the Kelly Medical Center. As an official Medical Center we are allowed some special exemptions. Do you need time to review those special exemptions?" "Yes, but for now please enlighten us as we will check the facts later."

1. "A medical center is responsible for the treatment advances for the population within a 360-degree radius of +- 150 miles. That includes west to Santa Rosa NM, north to Trinidad CO, east to Elk City OK, and south to Lubbock TX. To make it more realistic that is +- 50,000 people in Amarillo and another 15,000 in surrounding counties.

2. Advanced treatments includes vascular surgery, orthopedic repairs, urological procedures, neurology, oncology, radiation treatments, neurosurgery for brain tumors and hematomas, and treating polio paralysis. That kind of care not only needs doctors but a large ancillary staff to make the system work safely.

3. We have the support of our District Judge Toliver as I present this letter requesting that the Kelly Medical Center not be hampered by negligent drafting of key workers or essential doctors.

4. Lastly, we are soon embarking on a new venture. We will be accepting medical students in their last six months of training. That will also qualify us as a training center for doctors."

There was a long pause as the board's speaker said, "so you are quoting technicalities and fine print exemptions to avoid us drafting ancillary help and doctors?" "No Sir, we are trying to stop you from killing US residents by crippling a medical system that we took 35 years to build. Our residents are just as important as our boys going to war. It is up to you to find the correct path to give our soldiers what they need without sacrificing the local population. That is all we have to say on the subject and we are sticking to it. What will be will be!"

*

Walking back to the hospital, Brad couldn't wait so he said, "what is this about taking senior medical students and when were you planning to spring this on me?" "I just got a letter yesterday from Doctor Huxley. Apparently the increased admission to medical school, surgical training, and new areas of internal medicine specialties, has overloaded the training programs at their medical center. They are entertaining sending senior medical students to distant medical centers in Albuquerque, Oklahoma City, Denver, Houston, and us! But by word of mouth, our institution is highest on the list of requested outside training centers." "Really, so in what department would you accept students?" "Seven departments: Neurology, Neurosurgery, Oncology, General Surgery, Orthopedics, Urology, and Vascular.

Plus every student must spend one day a week in the Polio Center—especially the breathing room."

There was a long pause as Brad said, "is there an advantage for us adding such an intensive and dedicated training program?" "In the short run, probably not! In the long run, absolutely. We have expanded our hospital, added new departments, and we will grow. So where do you think we are going to get new docs to add to our growing programs?" "You're right, home grown is the answer. Those students will see our modern building, state-of-the-art treatments, and top of the line medical staff. They will either fall in love with our young nurses or with us. We won't have to beg docs, we'll have to try to pick the best and the ones with our mindset, heh?"

Brad took her hand and said, "I know I can be slow on the draw, but I finally see why you are truly 'The Hospital Steward!'"

***

The End
Epilogue to follow.

EPILOGUE

Hello, my name is Bruce Kelly, I am the grandson of Bradley Kelly and the son of James Kelly—the 3rd generation. It is now 1964 and my son Willard, 4th generation, is about to enter medical school. Let me present the hospital's evolution over decades and will then discuss specific individuals.

First of all I am certain you are wondering what ever happened after the meeting with the draft board. Well I recall that no one was drafted out of the hospital. Instead, the draft board designated the Kelly Medical Center as a VA affiliate to assist veterans with rehab for their war injuries and amputations.

My grandmother's idea of paid educational day events were popular. It did not take a rocket scientist to realize that the program provided a regular referral of patients in all fields, as the three original fields of prostate surgery, brain tumors, and Parkinsons attracted the bulk of the referrals. Yet, that is not what kept the hospital prosperous. It was the medical school satellite training program. As the hospital grew, graduates in internal medicine specialties and specialized surgery were easily found.

Medicine changed drastically in the 50s and 60s. Cardiology now offered open heart surgery for failing valves and coronary artery bypass. Neurology now provided specific treatments for a myriad of disorders, Oncology now had an extensive array of chemotherapeutic agents, kidney disease had advanced to dialysis, radiation therapy had a more directed radiation beam, and brain imaging finally came into play. Neurosurgery had progressed to incredibly high-tech levels. Medical treatments had advanced with the new FDA approved drugs. Anesthesia had added spinal anesthesia as well as a group of halothane inhalational gases given under endotracheal intubation. Cardiology had added an extensive array of new drugs to control arrythmias, CHF, coronary artery disease, and heart attacks.

Keeping up with modern changes became a chore. Fortunately, grandma was able to start a visiting professor program to discuss new aspects in medicine and surgery. Now for some personal facts.

The Original Duo

Grandpa had to stop performing surgery at 65 because of cataracts. He and Grandma continued working as administrators till they were in their seventies. Today, they have moved to the Mexican border in a small town called Alamo Texas. They have developed several hobbies to occupy their time with new friends and they show no signs of slowing down. The family is worried about their chances of getting sick so far from home and wonder if they shouldn't think of spending their time in Amarillo year-round. Their thoughts to that are: "If we are in Amarillo year-round we'll end up working or be a bother. This way we live away five months a year and when home, we play and read to pass the time. Afterall, with commercial jets we can travel the 700 miles from Alamo to Amarillo in two hours—big deal. For emergencies, we have several good hospitals right here in the Rio Grande Valley."

The Second-Generation Duos

Aunt Dottie and Uncle Eric had perfect careers. It was our aunt who said it best, "every day is such a pleasure. We go to work in a beautiful building, deal with modern medicine and surgery, enjoy the patients, the wonderful workers, and medical staff. Dottie always stayed close to the breathing center and the polio victims, but over the years, she became the well-known oncologist that was in charge of the department after Doc Nichols retired. When Doc Greene retired, they replaced him with two docs: a pathologist with lab tech-savvy, and a truly certified radiation therapist. Dottie's career was closely tied with the new Doc Winters as they often mixed radiation and chemotherapy concurrently or separately per protocol.

Dad had a busy surgical practice. As the head of the surgical department he was mostly involved in vascular surgery as well as neurosurgery—as the two specialties were often intertwined. With vascular imaging, he was able to provide peripheral bypasses to avoid amputations because of occlusive vascular disease. It was Eric Hall who said, "to see Jimmy dissecting a brain tumor is a miracle in progress." Fortunately, mom's talent in identifying a brain site, that was the cause for symptoms, made dad's work much easier. Our uncle Eric was the perfect assistant in neurosurgical cases, but in time he became the renowned urologist as master of the non-invasive techniques.

Now to tie up loose-ends, let me give you some follow-up on characters that became regular individuals tied to the Kelly Medical Center.

Louisa. Worked from the early 30s till the breathing center was closed in 1963. Married to Roland the orderly, they had three kids, and managed to be in the breathing center when she went into labor for all three births. On her retirement in 1963 she was given a $10,000 gift from our grandparents.

Doc Norwood. There was another tough one to bring to the retirement status. He delivered his last baby at age 70 and retired in Amarillo.

Mister Gregory. Believe it or not, he is 90+ years old, still keeps in touch with his favorite hospital, and is still slipping some 'tips' to the current hospital administrator.

That brings us to the third generation, me and my brother William. Unfortunately he and I never inherited the medical gene. Instead we both went into business. William is a successful manager of a trust fund and I went into hospital administration. Yes, I am the Kelly Medical Center current administrator. Following my grandparents' footsteps is a real challenge. Our hospital is now on the fourth floor and the engineers are designing new technology to extend it two more floors. We now have a daily occupancy of 200 patients, and have a medical staff of 32 doctors. Instead of fighting with the local city council for a subsidy, we now fight with Medicare, Medicaid, BC-BS, and other private insurance companies. To make it worse, we now have a state organization that controls prices we can charge patients and insurances. But as my grandparents managed thru WWI, the 1918 flu, the Great Depression, the Polio epidemic, WWII, and the Korean War; we shall manage as well. Today we are dealing with the Vietnam War as the medical world is still trying to cure cancer, find a treatment for these infectious viruses that plague the world, and NASA is saying we will land on the moon before the turn of this decade.

In closing, I am certain that you saw what demands were on our past hospital stewards. And so, the current demands on a hospital steward continue as a sign of the times.

Respectfully submitted,
Bruce Kelly, CEO
Kelly Medical Center

ABOUT THE AUTHOR

The author is a retired medical physician who, with his wife of 50+ years, spend their summers in Vermont and their winters in the Texas Rio Grande Valley.

Early in his retirement before 2016, he enjoyed his lifelong hobby of guns and shooting. He participated in the shooting sports to include Cowboy Action Shooting, long range black powder, USPSA, trap, and sporting clays. At the same time he wrote a book on shooting a big bore handgun, a desk reference on volume reloading, and two fictions on the cowboy shooting sports. Since 2016 he has become a prolific writer of western fiction circa 1870-1900—the Cowboy Era.

It was during the Covid pandemic, in a self-imposed quarantine, that he wrote a dozen books. A newly adopted writing genre covered three phases: a bounty hunter's life as a Paladin with his unique style of bringing outlaws to justice, a romantic encounter that changed his life, and the building of a lifelong enterprise that would support the couple's future when they hanged up their guns—as each enterprise is different from book to book.

Although three of his books have a sequel, the others are all a standalone publication. With a dozen books ready for publication in 2023, and to keep the subject matter varied, this author elects to publish them out of sequence.

I hope you enjoy reading my books, and if you do, please leave a comment on the seller's web site.

Richard M Beloin MD

AUTHOR'S PUBLICATIONS

Non fiction

Fiction in modern times

Western fiction (circa 1880-1900+)
(The Bounty Hunter/Entrepreneur series)

Western Fiction (circa 1873-1933)
(The Bounty Hunter, Romance
and entrepreneur series)

Western Fiction (circa 1900-1930)
Romance and Entrepreneur